"What part of 'I don't lie' is unclear to you?"

It was apparent that his supply of patience was seriously running low.

Sam blew out a breath. "No part," she freely admitted. It wasn't that she didn't understand what Mike was claiming—she just didn't know whether she actually believed him. "I just never met anyone who didn't, let's say, 'bend the truth' once in a while when it was to their advantage."

"Well, now you have." He gave her a penetrating look that was meant to intimidate her. It annoyed him that it failed and yet it was also the start of grudging respect for her feistiness. "Are you going to argue with me all the way into town, or are you finally going to stop looking a gift horse in the mouth and just accept the fact that you lucked out?" he asked.

A few choice hot words rose to her lips, but she managed to keep them under wraps. Someday, though, she promised herself, she and this man were going to have it out—and she would put him in his place the way no one else apparently ever did.

Dear Reader,

I cannot remember when I first became fascinated by the various cultures of the first inhabitants of North America. I've been told that it seems to be a hallmark of foreign-born citizens to embrace Westerns. Me, I embraced the underdog in those Westerns. I was into learning about Native Americans way before it was popular, at a time when they were still known as Indians and no one realized that Custer provoked the confrontation at Little Big Horn because he wanted to be seen as a brave hero by the country. His goal was to be elected president the way Grant had been.

But I digress (occupational habit). When I was in fifth grade, I read a book called *White Squaw,* about a wife and mother who was kidnapped by Indians and eventually returned to her family. That story has stayed with me all these years. I thought it might be interesting if Mike Rodriguez decided to have someone organize and transcribe his great-great-great-grandmother's journals so his own grandchildren would be firmly connected to their roots. As luck would have it, Mike's ancestor was kidnapped by the natives of the area. And, as luck would also have it, the ghostwriter whom he hires to create a book from the journals is a widow searching for roots herself. By the time she has organized the journals into a coherent whole, she winds up capturing Mike's heart and he hers. Happy endings all around. (What? You were expecting maybe not?)

As always I thank you for reading. I take none of you for granted and hope I have succeeded in entertaining you. From the bottom of my heart, I wish you someone to love who loves you back.

All my best,

Marie

A SMALL TOWN THANKSGIVING

—

MARIE FERRARELLA

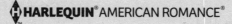

HARLEQUIN® AMERICAN ROMANCE®

Recycling programs
for this product may
not exist in your area.

ISBN-13: 978-0-373-75479-3

A SMALL TOWN THANKSGIVING

Copyright © 2013 by Marie Rydzynski-Ferrarella

All rights reserved. Except for use in any review, the reproduction or utilization of this work in whole or in part in any form by any electronic, mechanical or other means, now known or hereafter invented, including xerography, photocopying and recording, or in any information storage or retrieval system, is forbidden without the written permission of the publisher, Harlequin Enterprises Limited, 225 Duncan Mill Road, Don Mills, Ontario M3B 3K9, Canada.

This is a work of fiction. Names, characters, places and incidents are either the product of the author's imagination or are used fictitiously, and any resemblance to actual persons, living or dead, business establishments, events or locales is entirely coincidental.

This edition published by arrangement with Harlequin Books S.A.

For questions and comments about the quality of this book, please contact us at CustomerService@Harlequin.com.

® and TM are trademarks of Harlequin Enterprises Limited or its corporate affiliates. Trademarks indicated with ® are registered in the United States Patent and Trademark Office, the Canadian Trade Marks Office and in other countries.

Printed in U.S.A.

ABOUT THE AUTHOR

Marie Ferrarella, a USA TODAY bestselling and RITA® Award–winning author, has written more than two hundred books for Harlequin, some under the name Marie Nicole. Her romances are beloved by fans worldwide. Visit her website, www.marieferrarella.com.

Books by Marie Ferrarella

HARLEQUIN AMERICAN ROMANCE

HARLEQUIN ROMANTIC SUSPENSE

SILHOUETTE ROMANTIC SUSPENSE

HARLEQUIN SPECIAL EDITION

SILHOUETTE SPECIAL EDITION

*Cavanaugh Justice
**The Doctors Pulaski
†Kate's Boys
††The Fortunes of Texas: Return to Red Rock
‡The Baby Chase
‡‡‡Matchmaking Mamas
=The Fortunes of Texas: Lost…and Found
‡‡Forever, Texas
^Montana Mavericks: The Texans Are Coming!
#The Fortunes of Texas: Whirlwind Romance
-Montana Mavericks: Back in the Saddle
***The Fortunes of Texas: Southern Invasion
%The Coltons of Wyoming

To Nik,
Who Finally
Got It All Together
And Got It
Right

Prologue

The day began like all the days that had come before. It was too hot with too much to do and none of it to my liking. I was bored and yearning for excitement, for an adventure that would take me away from trying to coax a bit of green, a bit of growth out of the parched, dry ground that destroyed more than it yielded.

I was young and wanted to live before I was old and dried up before my time, like Abuela and Tia Josefina. Tia and Abuela came to live with Papa after Mama died. Papa said she died bringing me into the world. I have no way of knowing if that is true since she was gone by the time I started to remember things. But Papa does not lie, so I suppose it must be so.

Frustrated with my futile efforts in the garden, I went to fetch water from the stream that ran on our property. Anything to get away from the boredom and the hard work, if only for a moment.

The stream is always cool and I can take my shoes and stockings off so I can feel the water against my sweating skin.

Sometimes, when I go to the stream, I pretend I am a princess, held against my will, waiting for a prince to come rescue me and take me away to his castle in *the mountains. I pretend so hard that once or twice, I thought I heard the whinny of a horse and the sound of hooves against the ground.*

I am disappointed when I look to see that the sound belongs to my imagination. Or to a stray mustang running closer than he should.

There are horses here that have no masters, that run where they want to and are freer than I am. I envy them. Or I did before...

But since that afternoon, I find myself longing for the boredom of home, for the tedious labor of scratching the ground, coaxing life from the hard, dry soil. For the feeling of triumph the few times I succeeded. When you lose something, that is the time when you realize that you really wanted it and did not have the sense to value it when it was yours.

But that day, when I went to fetch the water and dreamed of princes searching for their princess, the sound of horses existed outside my imagination. They existed in the real world.

The sound belonged to the Indian ponies that came galloping at me. Indian ponies mounted with riders. When I saw them coming, I ran as if the very devil was after me because he was. Abuela and Tia and Papa all warned me to be careful, that the Mescalero-Apaches would just as soon kill us than look at us. Papa said that they thought we invaded their land. When I asked him if we had, he told me that we were making it better, but that they did not understand that. I think they do not understand that because we do not speak their language and they do not speak ours.

I was swift of foot and could beat my brothers whenever we ran, but I was not swifter than an In-

*dian and one of the riders caught me and picked me up
as easily as I could pick up one of Tia's baby chicks.*

*I begged him to put me down and the rider yelled
something to another rider and then at me, but I could
not understand.*

*For the first time in my fourteen years, I thought
about dying for I was more frightened than I could
ever recall being.*

*I prayed for God to welcome me and to make my
dying less painful.*

LETTING OUT A long breath, Miguel Rodriguez stared at
the faded ink in the worn book he had just discovered
and been reading for the past half hour. The pages of
the book were so dry they fairly crackled beneath his
fingers as he turned them. Afraid they might tear, he
was handling them as gently as humanly possible for
a man with hands the size and thickness of leather
catchers' mitts.

The book was one of half a dozen or more such
tattered, cloth-covered journals he had just uncovered in his attic.

He had come up to the attic driven by a sudden
desire to put his house in order figuratively and literally, something he'd felt compelled to do since suffering a heart attack earlier in the year. The unexpected
event had unceremoniously brought him to the brink
of his existence and taught him how truly fragile life
was—as if he really needed that lesson since his beloved wife had passed on all these years ago.

But with his sons Miguel, Jr. and Ramon caring
for his ranch and his other four offspring volunteering sporadically whenever they had the time, Miguel

found he had a lot of free time to himself now. Never one who could handle too much free time well, he decided to get busy and turned his attention to things that had long been neglected.

Things like the attic, where nonessential items far too precious to part with at the moment were sent to await a verdict about their future.

Unfortunately, "out of sight, out of mind" seemed the golden rule for dealing with the attic and he had forgotten about over half the things that had been stored up there over the years. Some he barely remembered even *after* having spent the past few days browsing through the storage boxes.

This particular box, however, contained the journals that he couldn't remember ever having looked through before.

Vaguely, as he thought back now, Miguel thought he recalled his mother giving the battered old container to him more than fifty years ago, saying something about passing it on to the next generation to preserve. His mother had mentioned that they were stories that had been written by his great-great-great-grandmother, Marguerite Perez-Rodriguez.

At the time, he now remembered, he'd thought that his mother was talking about short stories, that the box contained some sort of a creative writing endeavor attempted by his long-departed ancestor.

But looking at the journal in his hand now, he was beginning to suspect that perhaps his mother had meant that they were memoirs or recollections from his great-great-great-grandmother's youth, not some sort of stories she had made up.

Sitting here now, a lantern turned up to its maximum capacity to banish the darkness from that one corner of the attic, Miguel ran his hand along the journal's tattered spine with reverence, as if he was touching something very precious.

For all the world, he felt as if he had just stepped into the past. A past that connected him to his family, to his roots and, in an odd sort of way, to the future and to the children who had yet to come.

His unborn grandchildren.

An idea suddenly came to him, taking hold of his imagination. The more he thought about it, the more pleased he became.

But if this was going to happen, he needed help.

Miguel sat there in the stillness and the aging dust, trying to think of who he might turn to with this, who could advise him who he should seek out in order to get started on this journey into the Rodriguez past.

And then he smiled as a name occurred to him.

For once, it wasn't one of his children.

Chapter One

Miguel Rodriguez Jr. referred to as "Mike" by everyone but his father, frowned as he sat in the cluttered room that his father referred to as his study, listening to Miguel Sr. tell him about his latest plan, the one involving not the ranch but the ranch *house*.

Mike could feel his frown deepening with each word that his father uttered.

When the older Rodriguez paused because he was either finally finished or—more likely—just taking a breath, Mike saw his opportunity to register and give voice to his displeasure at this newest turn of events.

"You know, Dad, this keeps up and whenever the occasional tourist passes through Forever, asking where the local hotel is, people'll just start sending them in this direction."

Six months ago had seen his father inviting Valentine Jones, a movie location scout who thought their property would be perfect for her studio's next film, to stay at their house for part of the shoot. That had turned out fairly well, especially for Rafe, but that had been a fluke. The thought of another stranger living here at the house left Mike cold.

He didn't really mind strangers, but he wanted

them in his own terms. And he did value his privacy—a great deal.

"*Why* are we putting up this person again?" he grumbled at his father.

"Because, as you so wisely pointed out, my beloved oldest son," Miguel said expansively, rocking back in his chair, "there *is* no hotel here in Forever. The woman who has agreed to go over those diaries and journals that I found in the attic needs to stay somewhere while she works."

Mike supposed what his father said was logical, but as far as he was concerned, it was also logical not to get in the habit of welcoming strangers with open arms. At times it was hard enough having not just four brothers and a sister, but their various spouses, moving through the house. Adding an unfamiliar face to the mix was flirting with the proverbial straw that had brought such grief to the camel and his back.

"Never said she didn't," Mike pointed out. "But why does it have to be here?" His dark eyes narrowed as he repeated a well-known fact. "I don't like strangers traipsing through the ranch."

"Once you meet her, she will no longer be a stranger," Miguel told his son, echoing an optimistic, upbeat philosophy he strongly believed in. "And since she will be working on your great-great-great-grandmother's journals, it is only right that she stay here. That way, if she has any questions," Miguel explained, "she will not have far to go for an answer."

Mike knew it was futile to point out that there were such magic devices as telephones and their brethren that could easily handle any questions that might come up. Instead, he went on record and voiced a lament.

"You know, Dad, I liked it a lot better when we were all struggling to keep one jump ahead of the bill collectors and you didn't have time for any fancy projects that had us holding an open house. What's next?" Mike asked. "We turn the house into a bed-and-breakfast?"

His oldest had a decent heart, but Miguel Jr. had never been accused of being overly friendly. For the most part, he kept to himself. He could be counted on in an emergency, but had a tendency to disappear when all was going well. He wasn't one, Miguel thought now, who liked to stop and smell the roses. His first-born was more inclined to walk right over the roses because as far as he was concerned, the flowers didn't serve any practical purpose.

"Having Valentine here did not turn out so badly, now, did it?" Miguel asked, tilting his head slightly in order to look into his son's face. He was hoping for a glimmer of a smile. He saw none.

"We lucked out that time," Mike countered with a careless shrug. And by his reckoning, they had run out of luck. "She married Rafe and they're happy, I get that. But Val had said that she wasn't going to stay for more than a week. From everything that you just said, this one is going be moving in with us until we all grow old and die," he grumbled.

"She's not going to be here long," Miguel protested, "just until she has your great-great—"

Mike's hand shot up as if to push the vocalization of the woman's full lineage back. His patience was at a premium and that premium didn't include having to listen to an endless repetition of the word *great*.

"Please, Dad," Mike begged, "just say G-4 or

something like that. I'm well aware that she was really 'great.'"

Always willing to do what he could within reason to humor his children, Miguel obliged. "Just until she organizes G-4's journals so that she can transcribe them all into a single book."

Mike had glanced at the journals the first night his father had brought the dusty, dilapidated box down from the attic, bursting with excitement over what he'd found. As far as he was concerned, what his father had so dismissively described as organizing probably involved an enormous amount of work. But maybe he was wrong. He was more than willing to find out that he was.

"And how long is *that* going to take?" Mike asked.

"I don't know, son," Miguel confessed honestly. "This is all new to me."

Mike stifled a sigh. Just as he thought. "Exactly," he said out loud. "How do you know she won't be taking advantage of your hospitality? She might decide to stick around endlessly." The last thing they needed, he thought, was a pseudo-intellectual lolling around, spouting a few learned words and then withdrawing into her room to live off them for another day.

Damn it, he wasn't going to let his father get duped this way, Mike thought.

"How do you know she will be?" his father countered innocently.

His father's heart was just too good and too big, Mike silently lamented. "Because it's human nature to take advantage of people."

"Forever is filled with people," Miguel reminded

his son. "And they," he went on proudly, "do not take advantage of one another."

For the most part, Mike knew he couldn't argue with that. But that kind of behavior was not the norm. The world was filled with con artists and scammers. Their little town was the exception to the rule. "Forever is an unusual place."

"And maybe, once she is here, this woman will be just as 'unusual' as everyone else in Forever," his father theorized. "Give the woman a chance, boy," Miguel requested. His eyes washed over his son, silently entreating Mike to lighten up. Not for the sake of the young woman who hadn't arrived yet, but for his own sake. Miguel felt that his son was missing out on so much being like this. "You have to be more open-hearted, Miguel."

Mike shook his head. In his opinion, his father's heart was *much* too open. "And just where did you get this woman's name?" he asked.

Ordinarily, along with the question, he would have thrown in a warning about using anything that came off an online site because as far as he was concerned, his father was incredibly innocent for a man his age. But his father didn't even have a nodding acquaintance with a computer or the internet and no desire to strike up any sort of friendship with either anytime soon. So the idea of his father surfing through want ads was just incredibly ludicrous.

Thank God for small favors, Mike thought wryly.

But the question still remained: Where had he found this woman's name?

"Olivia recommended her," Miguel answered simply.

Mike stared at his father, almost dumbfounded. "Olivia?"

Miguel nodded his dark head. "The sheriff's wife."

Mike closed his eyes for a second, searching for strength. "I know who Olivia is, Dad. I'm just surprised that she would condone something like this." As far as he knew, Olivia was a private person. Perhaps not as private as he was, but relatively close. Why would she just give him someone's name like that? What did she know about this woman? And who could vouch for this so-called journal organizer?

"She didn't just condone it," Miguel informed him proudly. "She encouraged it. *And,*" he said with emphasis, saving the best for last, "she thinks my idea of passing this book on to my grandchildren when it is finished is a very good idea."

A sense of defeat pressed against his chest. Mike could see that his father had made up his mind about this. He knew that once that happened, there was no swaying the old man. Miguel Rodriguez was an easygoing, loving man most of the time. He could also be as stubborn as hell once he set his mind on something, Mike thought with an inward sigh.

Granted, the ranch was supposed to belong to all of them equally, but it was an unspoken rule that Miguel got the final say in all matters should there be a division of opinion. After all, this had been Miguel Rodriguez's ranch before he had decided to divide the land among all of them. It had been his way of thanking his children for pitching in to save the ranch from its creditors and the bank that sought to foreclose on it. Had they not all found some sort of work and handed every penny they earned over to him, the ranch would currently belong to another family, not theirs.

Throwing in the towel, Mike decided he needed to get the particulars nailed down so that at least he knew how long he had to put up with this so-called intellectual's invasion.

He pinned his father with a look. "Exactly how long is Miss Organizer going to be here?"

Miguel had always tried to be truthful with his children, never answering something for the sake of closing the subject if he actually didn't know. "That depends."

"On what?" Mike's voice rose with a touch of indignation. "On whether or not she likes getting a free ride?"

Mike knew for a fact that his father's hospitality was boundless, that whoever stayed here on the ranch wouldn't be allowed to contribute a dime toward their keep and while his family was far from financially hurting these days, he didn't like the idea of his father being taken advantage of by some little two-bit opportunist, either.

Miguel gave no indication that his son's tone annoyed him. "On how long it will take her to organize those journals and diaries in such a way that she can use them to create a memoir that does your great-great—that does G-4 justice," Miguel amended.

Mike didn't bother stifling his sigh of displeasure this time. "In other words, she's going to become a permanent member of the household."

"Only if you or Ramon marry her," his father countered innocently. "The way Rafe married Valentine."

Or if you marry her, Mike thought, keeping the

response, which he meant more than half-seriously, to himself. It had been a long time since his mother had died and there were times Mike worried that his father was ripe for the picking by some enterprising little gold digger.

"Well, I certainly won't," Mike said out loud, "and Ray is still half pining after that starlet who was here while they were filming that movie in Forever. Although he does fall in and out of love like some people change socks," Mike acknowledged, "so maybe you'd better warn this literary cleaning lady that she might just want to stay where she is instead of coming to the Casa de Rodriguez," Mike concluded.

His father surprised him by shaking his head sadly and asking, "When did it happen, *mi hijo?*"

Mike looked at his father, confused. "When did what happen?"

"When did you become this old man?" Miguel asked. "These are the years when you are supposed to be young and foolish, my son. Enjoy life. Make mistakes and pick yourself up and try again. That is how you grow," the older man insisted. "Through experiences."

Sure there might have been times—few though they were, Mike silently maintained—when he thought that something might be missing from his life. But that had been part of the sacrifice he'd felt he had to make for the good of the family. "Sorry, Dad. Someone around here has to be the serious one."

The way Miguel saw it, it was a matter of definition. "There is serious and then there is inflexible." Miguel patted his son's face. "Do not miss out on being young, Miguel. You only get one chance at it."

He was who he was and for the most part, he'd made his peace with that. He was too old to change now, Mike thought. "You seem to be doing just fine for both of us, Dad."

Miguel shook his head. It was obvious by his expression that he was trying to understand just where he had gone wrong, where he had failed his first-born. All his other children were outgoing and had a zest for life, even Eli, while Miguel Jr. seemed to work hard at avoiding it, foregoing any personal dealings outside the family—sometimes even *inside* the family. That was no way to live, the older man thought sadly.

But it wasn't a problem that could be solved quickly, or even soon. And he had something more pressing that needed tending to.

"We can discuss this at some other time," Miguel told his son. "Right now I need you to go and pick the young lady up at the airport."

The closest airport to Forever was over fifty miles away. A trip of that nature would take a huge chunk out of his day.

"When?" Mike asked, preparing to beg off whatever date his father gave him.

"Leaving in the next twenty minutes would be nice." Miguel watched his son's jaw drop in amazement. "I know how you like to give yourself enough time in case something comes up like a traffic jam outside of Laredo."

"Today?" Mike asked in disbelief. "You want me to pick her up *today?*"

Miguel nodded. "Her plane lands in a little less than two hours."

"And you're just telling me this now?" Mike asked in disbelief.

"I thought it was better that way. It gives you less time to be angry about it. You know how you get," he pointed out sadly to his son.

"Dad, I can't just drop everything and—"

"You have nothing to drop," Miguel told him calmly. "I have already checked."

Mike didn't like being thought of as predictable. "What if I had plans you didn't know about?" he challenged.

"When have you ever had plans no one knew about?" his father countered.

"I could," Mike maintained stubbornly.

"Do you?" Miguel asked, his eyes meeting his son's.

With reluctance and no small measure of annoyance, Mike replied, "No, I don't."

"Good, then I would hurry if I were you."

"How am I supposed to find this literary genius?" he wanted to know.

It was more a matter of the young woman finding his son, Miguel thought. After he'd seen her picture, thanks to Olivia's computer, he saw great potential— not just for his ancestor's journals, but for his present- day son, as well.

"I told her you would hold up a sign with her name on it and I described you to her."

Mike stared at his father. "You *knew* I was going to pick her up?" He'd just agreed to it this moment. He could have just as easily said no and refused, Mike thought.

"Of course," Miguel replied complacently. "I am

your father. I know everything. I told her to look for a tall, dark, handsome man with a deep scowl on his face. Of course, if you have the sign with her name on it, it would not really confuse the young woman if you were, perhaps, smiling," his father concluded hopefully.

"Maybe not, but it might confuse me," Mike quipped. And then he sighed. "What's her name so I can write it on the sign?"

"Her name is Samantha Monroe," his father told him. Reaching behind the sofa, Miguel pulled out a large white poster board he'd prepared earlier. Both the woman's name as well as his own was on it. And beneath that was the name of their ranch.

The lettering was rather distinctive and very eye-catching. That did *not* look like his father's handiwork, Mike couldn't help thinking.

"You did this?" Mike asked rather skeptically.

Miguel laughed softly under his breath even as he shook his head. "I would like to take the credit for it, but it was Tina, Olivia's sister, who is the artistic one."

"Tina," Mike repeated. "Olivia's sister," he added for good measure. "Did everybody in town know about this woman coming but me?"

"Not everybody," his father replied evasively. "Just those who would not be upset by the news."

"In other words, everyone but me," Mike repeated.

He blew out a breath, annoyed because he knew he was on the losing end of a disagreement that he had been destined to lose before he was ever born. Mike freely acknowledged that he was different from his brothers and his sister in that by no stretch of the imagination could he be described as being sociable, ready to call any stranger "friend" after an exchange of only a few words. Pressing his lips together, he kept his comment to himself. Instead, he reached for the sign and muttered, "I'll see you later."

His father followed him to the door. "Thank you, Miguel."

Mike made no answer. He didn't trust himself to say anything at all. Instead, he merely nodded in response and kept on walking.

PACKING WAS EASY when you had very little to pack, and possessions had never been a big factor in Samantha Monroe's life.

So, picking up and physically being ready to travel was no problem.

Acclimating was more difficult.

Sam had butterflies in her stomach. The same butterflies that showed up each and every time she began a new project. There was that fear that she wasn't up to the job and the fear of having to travel alone to unfamiliar places.

Before she had undertaken this career, she had never seen the outside of her little suburban Maryland town. She'd had twenty-five years of moving along the same streets, nodding at the same neighbors and being completely devoid of any desire to see anything beyond those boundaries.

Those were hard things to give up.

But she had to.

With Danny gone, a bank account amounting to seventeen dollars and twelve cents and bills to pay, Sam knew she had no other choice. She had no way to take care of herself if she remained inert.

Danny had been the very light of her life, but he hadn't exactly been the kind who believed in saving for a rainy day. He believed in spending every dime as long as the sun was shining.

Which was exactly what happened when he went on that February skiing trip with his two best friends. Promising to be "back before you know it," he went off for a carefree weekend of fun.

He hadn't counted on an encounter with a tanker truck whose cross-country driver had pushed himself too hard and had fallen asleep behind the wheel. The truck careened out of control and despite Danny's frantic attempts to get the car out of harm's way, there had been a collision. It ultimately turned out not to be as serious as it could have been—but just serious enough for one fatality—Danny's.

His two friends and the sleeping driver survived the crash.

And so, a little more than eighteen months after becoming a bride, she had become a widow. A widow with bills and no way to pay them. There were no parents for her to fall back on or turn to, no parents around at all. Her father had never been in the picture, vanishing months before she was born, and her mother had worked endless hours to provide for the two of them. When she wasn't working, her mother was searching for "Mr. Right," someone to take them away from the brink of poverty where they had always existed.

However, when her mother finally found that man, he only took her away. And Sam was left behind. By then, she had turned eighteen and was officially on her own, the way she had been, unofficially, for most of her life.

But she wasn't alone, not really. Danny had lived across the street and had been part of her life since she'd had her first memory.

Before even that.

They were friends, and then sweethearts and then lovers who were destined to get married. When they did, Sam was truly ready for a happily-ever-after life—as much as any life could be happily-ever-after.

But fate had other ideas and fate always won out in the end. So, at twenty-seven, she found herself very much alone and determined to hold her head up high. The latter entailed providing for herself. All she needed was the way how.

Sam loved biographies and had always had the ability to put words together eloquently on a page. She eventually combined her passion and talent to become a ghostwriter. A much sought-after ghostwriter because she also had the ability to mimic any voice, sound like any person who hired her to do the heavy lifting and tell the story of their life.

In addition, she had an aptitude for knowing what interested readers and a neat, clean style that delivered what had been promised while leaving the so-called autobiographer's ego intact.

Her chosen career necessitated travel, which in turn required a certain independence she was only now growing accustomed to. Eventually, she hoped to be comfortable with flying to parts unknown at a moment's notice.

Right now, Sam thought as she deplaned amid a flock of passengers, she needed to find her new employer, for while the publishing house paid her salary, the person whose autobiography she would be fashioning was her boss. It was something she didn't ever forget and that one small trick was responsible for her working as steadily as she had been these past two years.

Joan, the main publisher's assistant at Tatum House, had told her to be on the lookout for her driver. The man had been described as tall, dark and handsome. He was also said to be scowling, although about what Joan hadn't a clue. The person who had called her hadn't covered that detail.

So there she was, walking in slow motion and taking in both sides of the area as best she could. The person, Joan had promised, would be holding a sign with her name on it.

So there was hope.

Bingo, Sam thought as she zeroed in on a man who fit the description she'd been given to a T.

And he was holding a large sign with her name written on it.

Doctor Livingston, I presume, she thought to herself as she began to forge a path toward the man who hadn't made eye contact with her yet.

Chapter Two

"Excuse me, are you Miguel Rodriguez?"

The melodic voice cut through the layers of tangled thoughts going through Mike's mind. When he turned to look at the source of the voice, his mind was still struggling to focus, fighting its way out of a fantasy-filled zone. He was imagining the woman he'd been sent to meet, picturing a matronly lady right down to a pair of sensible shoes and a tailored, unflattering suit.

Instead, the woman addressing him looked like what he would have conjured up after encountering a genie in a bottle. The petite young blonde standing before him would have constituted his first wish—and quite possibly just about every wish that he'd ever had.

"Yes. Yes, I am," he replied, the inside of his mouth unaccountably turning bone-dry. So much so that it felt as if any second now, he would start exhaling dust. "How did you know?" he heard himself asking.

She smiled up at him, causing his heart to momentarily stop before it suddenly started beating double time, all within the scope of approximately fifteen seconds. Her sky-blue eyes teasingly captured his as she pointed to the rectangular piece of cardboard he'd forgotten he was holding in his hands.

"That kind of gave me a clue," she told him. "You're holding up my name," she explained when he made no effort to acknowledge what she'd just said

Mike blinked, slowly coming to. "I am? Oh, yeah, I am."

The next moment, as his own words—as well as Samantha Monroe's—sank in, he suddenly felt like a contestant for—and most likely the winner of—the crown of Jackass of the Decade.

Possibly of the century.

A massive wave of embarrassment washed over him.

He had no idea what had just come over him. It wasn't as if he'd never seen a beautiful woman before. His own sister, Alma, though he wouldn't have readily admitted it to her, was an extremely attractive young woman, as were the women that his brothers, Eli, Gabe and Rafe, had married.

But something about this woman, about the laughter in her eyes, her straight golden hair and her sexy figure sent an earthquake rippling through him. The sum total of those assets could have made a dead man sit up and beg.

"Well, since I found you, I think you can put the sign down now," Sam gently prompted.

"Yeah," Mike agreed, still stumbling over his tongue. That part of his anatomy seemed to have inexplicably grown in weight and girth.

"Funny," Sam went on to observe, "I pictured someone a bit older when I spoke to you on the phone the other day." There was amusement in her eyes as she told him, "You certainly don't look like the patriarch of such a large family."

"No, I d— Wait, what?" he asked, confusion running rampant through the fog that encircled his brain.

"I said I pictured someone older when I spoke to you the other day," Sam repeated.

She was fairly certain that there had to be some sort of a mistake. No matter which way you sliced it, the tall, handsome cowboy standing before her was *not* well into his fifth decade. She doubted if he was finished with his second one. Or, at the very most, had just gotten a toehold of his third.

But she was not about to shower this man with questions. She was giving him leeway to surrender any sort of an explanation. She had no intentions of crowding him or rushing him to clarify. To be honest, she found his verbal stumbling rather sweet and definitely flattering.

It had been a long time since anyone had looked at her as if she was an attractive female. Just because she earned a living as a ghostwriter did not mean that she was supposed to be invisible to the naked eye. Her last three clients had been women and while she could capture their perspective even better than she could that of a male client, she did like the almost involuntary appreciative look in this man's eyes.

For the most part, the women she'd worked with had acted as if she didn't really exist, but she supposed it was because they would have preferred that people think they had written their own autobiographies rather than that they'd had help in wording them. She amounted to their dirty little secret and as such had to be as close to nonexistent as possible.

"You didn't talk to me."

"I spoke to Miguel Rodriguez," Sam pointed out,

her cadence deliberately slow and easy, giving the man every opportunity to interrupt and set the record straight whenever he wanted. "And you did say that that was your name."

"It is," Mike agreed. "That's the name written on my birth certificate." But then he hastened to clarify the point. "But I'm Junior to my father's Senior."

She smiled. It wasn't as if she'd never encountered *that* before. "Is that what you'd like me to call you?" she asked. "Junior?"

He didn't look like a Junior anything. Tall, with wide shoulders, rather appealing small waist and hips, with wavy, thick black hair that made her fingers unexpectedly itchy, he was definitely in a class all his own.

"Mike," he told her, his voice striking a note of command. "Call me Mike."

"Mike," she repeated, her smile once again mesmerizing him and all but freezing his brain, making it impossible for him to form a coherent thought. "I like that."

"Yeah, me, too." The words fell flat and were incredibly lame.

What was going on with him? Mike silently demanded of himself. He'd never sounded like a blithering idiot before, not even in the presence of a drop-dead knockout like that starlet that Ray was so crazy about.

Why was this particular woman numbing his brain and completely negating his ability to think in near complete sentences?

"And what do I call you?" he asked, wanting to

say at least one semi-intelligent thing in her presence. "Ms. Monroe, or—"

"Sam," she told him, cutting off any further speculation on the cowboy's part. "Everyone just calls me Sam."

"Sam" was way too masculine-sounding a name for someone who was the absolute antithesis of masculinity, he couldn't help thinking. But she obviously seemed to like the name and for no other reason than to go along with whatever the woman wanted, Mike nodded and repeated the name.

"Sam."

Then, remembering that he was supposed to be a walking, talking, functioning adult, Mike forced himself to follow up the single word, and say something more.

"Let's get your baggage."

It came out more like a gruff order, but Mike preferred that to sounding like some mesmerized halfwit incapable of stringing four words together into a discernible whole.

"This is it," Sam informed him, indicating the two pieces of luggage she had with her. The larger piece was most obviously a suitcase on wheels, the kind that easily fit into overhead compartments on planes; the other case was much smaller and in all likelihood contained her laptop inside. A wide, fringed dark brown hobo purse hung off her shoulder.

"You don't have anything else coming down the chute onto the carousel?" he asked, surprised.

Sam shook her head, her straight chin-length golden hair swaying to and fro as if to reinforce her denial. "No, I travel light."

Mike took that to mean that the rest of her things were being shipped out—which only bore out what he'd complained about to his father: that the woman was going to be moving in indefinitely.

And while Sam was admittedly a great deal prettier than Ray, the brother who was still living at home, Mike had to admit that he still didn't really like the idea of having a stranger moving into their ranch house for an indefinite period of time. Indefinite sounded too much like "forever"—the eternity, not the town.

"The rest of your things being shipped out?" he asked her, an accusing note in his voice.

"There is no 'rest of my things,'" she told him, then added, "This is it," indicating her meager belongings with a quick sweep of her hand.

Mike stared at the suitcase. "How much can you fit in there?"

"Enough," she replied with a smile that was both tranquilizing and yet seemed to be able to get an unsuspecting heart racing at the same time.

It certainly did his.

The next moment, Mike cleared his throat and said, "Then I guess if we have everything, we'd better get going."

"I guess so," she agreed, doing her best to keep a straight face. She didn't want this man to think that she was laughing at him or having fun at his expense.

But she did flash a smile in his direction.

Without a word, Mike took possession of her suitcase from her and claimed the black faux-leather briefcase with his other hand.

Mike took exactly two steps before he abruptly

stopped walking and turned around to look at her. Not expecting the sudden halt, Sam managed to just barely catch herself just in time to keep from plowing straight into him.

"Is something wrong?" she asked him, doing her best to appear unaffected by this whole venture. Her tall, handsome driver had no way of knowing how many knots currently resided in her stomach and she was going to keep it that way.

"Do you know what you're getting into?" Mike asked.

Until he'd just said the words out loud, it hadn't even occurred to him to ask. But this Sam woman appeared delicate to him. Moreover, she looked like someone who was accustomed to having all the amenities that places like New York, Los Angeles, Dallas and cities of that size had to offer a woman like her.

Forever didn't even have a hotel and there was just one movie theater in town, known simply as The Theater, and it ran second-run movies. And while they weren't exactly backward here in Forever, they certainly weren't considered cutting-edge, either. Not by a really long shot.

A "crime spree" here meant that Donnie Taylor and his younger brother, Will, carved their initials on the sides of two barns, or spray-painted those initials on the sides of someone's garage.

There was nothing modern or even noteworthy about a town like Forever. And most of the people who lived here liked it that way.

"Yes, I'm going to be reading and organizing some journals and diaries written by one of your ancestors. Your father said that this woman had been carried off by some Native Americans and spent a year with them before managing to escape. I'm assuming that she couldn't write anything down in a journal while it was happening, but once she was able to return home, she put everything down on paper as best she could, doing it in such a way as to make it seem that it was happening as she wrote." She looked up at the cowboy's tanned face. "Did I get that right?"

The wide shoulders rose and fell in a careless shrug. "I don't know, I didn't look at the books."

Maybe it was his imagination, but Sam seemed both surprised and a bit confused by his answer. "Oh, but how could you help not looking through the books?" she asked him. Had she stumbled across something like that herself, she knew she wouldn't have closed her eyes until she'd read all—or at least most of it—herself.

But then, she had always been hungry for family connections, something she'd never really had outside of her mother.

The next moment, realizing that her question might have sounded somewhat condescending or judgmental, Sam quickly withdrew it.

"I'm sorry, I didn't mean anything by that," she apologized.

He shrugged off both her apology and the question that had come before it. "That's not what I'm referring to," Mike told the young blonde.

"Then what are you referring to?" she asked him pleasantly, giving every indication that she wanted to hear him out no matter what he had to say.

"I just wanted to make sure that you knew what this place was like. Forever, I mean," he clarified in case she wasn't following him. He was still tripping over his own tongue, he thought in disgust. "We don't have a hotel," he began.

Sam nodded. "I gathered that," she replied. "Your father very generously invited me to stay at the ranch while I worked. But then you're probably aware of that," she realized, thinking out loud.

"Yeah, I am," he told her, then went back to listing the town's shortcomings. He honestly didn't know if he was trying to chase her away with the facts, or telling her this so that she was forewarned as to what to expect now, while she was still fresh and hot on the idea of pursuing this restoration project. "There are no fancy restaurants here."

"I didn't come here to eat, I came to work," she pointed out simply.

Mike found himself being reeled in by the woman's smile, despite his best efforts not to be. He wondered if she even knew how magnetic that smile of hers was. The next moment, a mocking voice in his head asked, *How could she not?*

"All we've got is a diner," Mike told her, continuing to list what he assumed a stranger would see as Forever's shortcomings.

"That sounds more than adequate for anything I might want," Sam assured him.

Since he'd mentioned Miss Joan's—how could anyone spending more than ten minutes in Forever be oblivious to Miss Joan's?—he felt it only right to give a little equal time to the only place in town that served alcohol.

"There's a saloon if you feel the need to unwind," he heard himself telling her. He slanted a glance in her direction to see if this piece of information would be welcomed, or barely registered. It turned out to be the latter.

"Good to know," she murmured. "Although I probably won't be visiting it," Sam speculated. "I'll be too busy with the journals." She looked up at him again, waiting. "Anything else?"

He thought for a moment, then said, "There's no nightlife here."

She didn't know what he was getting at. She could only make an educated guess that he thought she was something she wasn't. That she required entertainment and special treatment, like she was "high maintenance."

Nothing could have been further from the truth— and Sam was proud of that fact.

But for now, she tried to set his mind at ease as best she could.

"Mr. Rodriguez, I'm not exactly sure what it is you're saying or what you expect me to be, but I was raised in a small town in Maryland where they rolled up the sidewalk at seven-thirty every night. I don't require a 'night life.' What I require is a comfortable work atmosphere and an occasional conversation with friendly, decent people, something I'm assuming won't be difficult to encounter here.

"Now, if you find any of that objectionable or believe that any of it wouldn't be to your father's liking, tell me now so we can iron all this out before I get down to work."

Mike frowned as he listened to her, unable to believe that a woman who looked the way this Sam person did would be satisfied with so little.

"You'll be bored," Mike predicted.

Sam smiled at him in response. A wide, amused, guileless smile that sent ripples of unnamed anticipation through his gut.

"I am never bored, Mr. Rodriguez," she told him. "If need be, I make my own entertainment. Now, is there anything else?" she asked.

He blew out a breath and picked up the suitcase handle again.

"No," he told her, then added as an afterthought, "You can call me Mike."

"Mike," she echoed with a pleased nod of her head. She'd found the first chink in the wall. Sam considered it her first victory.

The first of many, Sam promised herself.

Chapter Three

"This is really beautiful country," Sam commented as she stared out the window of Mike's truck.

They'd been driving for about half an hour and in that time, the rather stoic cowboy behind the steering wheel had said nothing. Oh, he'd grunted a couple of times in acknowledgment of something she had said, but only after she'd deliberately addressed the remark or question to him.

As far as forming actual words on his own, he'd stubbornly refrained from that.

Obviously, the man had used up his less than vast supply of vocabulary at the airport. Determined to get more than a noise in response, she tried again, hoping that commenting on a preferred topic would get the taciturn man to speak.

"It probably hasn't changed all that much since the first settlers came out here in their covered wagons," she speculated when he still said nothing. "It looks untouched," she added, glancing in Mike's direction. When he still gave no indication that he was going to comment on her observation, she piled on another word. "Pristine, even."

Mike snorted.

"What?" she asked, eager to prod him. "Did I say something wrong?"

He made another noise and she thought that was all the interaction there was going to be, in which case she had gotten more of a response from a squeaky floorboard. But then Mike surprised her.

"Pristine," Mike repeated with a mocking tone. "All except for the electrical wires and the phone wires that're buried underground," he pointed out crisply.

"All except for that," she agreed, doing her best to keep a straight face. But her tone betrayed her when she told him, "Some progress is actually a lovely thing, Mike." Was he the type who had little patience with any kind of modern advancements?

"Never said it wasn't," Mike replied, keeping his eyes on the road despite the fact that there was nothing moving in either direction and most likely wouldn't be for most of the drive back to his ranch. They were twenty-five miles into their journey and the only thing on the road was more road.

After the sparse exchange between them, there was more silence.

Sam suppressed a sigh. This man would have no trouble with solitary confinement, she thought. As for her, she didn't relish silence.

She gave conversation another try. Eventually, the man would have to do some talking, if only in self-defense.

"So, is it just you and your father on the ranch?" she asked him.

He spared her a look that was completely unfathomable. "What makes you say that?"

"No reason," Sam said with a careless shrug. "I

don't have anything to go on, really, so I thought I'd make a guess."

He glanced back at the road. Questions about this woman were beginning to pile up in his mind, but he deliberately shoved them to the side, telling himself he didn't care one way or another.

"You guessed wrong," he told her in a monotone.

"Obviously," she allowed good-naturedly. "Okay, why don't you fill me in?"

It seemed to her as if he turned his head in slow-motion to look at her. "On what?"

Since she knew nothing about him or his family, that left the door wide-open when it came to subject matter. She spread her hands wide to underscore her feeling.

"On anything you want to. Family dynamics. The average annual rainfall around here." She continued making suggestions since she wasn't getting any kind of a reaction from him. "What your favorite animal is—"

"What?" Mike turned to look at her again, his brow furrowed. "Why would you want to know that?"

Finally! she thought in triumph. She'd gotten a reaction.

"Because it would be a start," she told him honestly. "I'm not picky, Mike. I like to get to know the people I'll be dealing with and," she continued with emphasis, "I'm a good listener—but you're going to have to talk for me to have something to listen to."

Mike blew out a long breath and the silence continued. Just as Sam was starting to think that she'd completely lost him, she heard the tall, silent cowboy say in a low voice, "I've got four brothers and a sister, all younger. Only Ray, the youngest, still lives at the ranch—besides me," he amended. "I'm partial to my horse and I have no idea what the 'average' rainfall around here is. I just know if it's been a good year or a bad year. Anything else?" he asked, although, for the most part, he expected that what he'd just volunteered would be enough to satisfy her.

Looking back later, he realized that he should have known better. It was true that he hardly knew the woman, but he'd always been fairly good about picking up clues and nothing about this woman had suggested that she was the quiet type, given to meditating and being content with her own thoughts for company. He had a feeling that she was the type who probably thought that a brass band was understated.

As suspected, he didn't have long to wait for the torrent of questions to begin.

"What are your brothers' and sister's names? If they don't live on the ranch with you and your father, what line of work do they do? Are any of them married? What do they think of your father wanting to have his great-great-great-grandmother's journals and diaries turned into a memoir? And how could you not at least look through one of the journals once you knew about them?"

Overwhelmed by the questions and the speed with which they were emerging and flowing from her lips, Mike pulled the truck over to the side of the road and turned the engine off.

"Hold it!" he ordered.

The command jolted Sam into a moment of silence. But only for a moment. The next moment, she was back asking questions.

Or at least *a* question.

"Is something wrong?" Sam asked. She assumed that there had to be something wrong with the truck because why else would he have pulled over so abruptly?

"When I asked if there was anything else, I was being—" The proper word eluded him for a moment.

"Sarcastic?" Sam guessed as the situation suddenly dawned on her.

He supposed he had been, but he hadn't expected her to actually say it. Nor had he expected the tidal wave of words that had come at him. It had completely overwhelmed him.

"I didn't think I was sending out an invitation for the Spanish Inquisition," he countered.

"I wasn't expecting you to answer all the questions," she told him. "I was giving you a number of questions to choose from."

No, she wasn't, Mike thought. She wanted answers to all of them. He could tell by the look in the woman's eyes—eyes that were unnervingly blue and hypnotic.

As for answering her questions, the hell he would. All answers did for someone like Sam was create more questions.

"Shouldn't you have a career that would be more in keeping with that insatiable curiosity of yours?" he asked the woman. "Like a journalist, or better yet, a TV reporter?"

She had no use for the latter, not after what she'd lived through.

"You mean someone who sticks a microphone into people's worst moments and tries to shatter their privacy by asking the most invasive questions?" she asked, thinking of the reporter who had camped out on her doorstep, hoping to capture her reaction for the viewing public when she first heard about Danny's accident.

Ordinarily, she wasn't a violent person, but she'd hit the woman's microphone out of her hand before escaping to her car and driving away. She'd cried for almost half an hour after that.

"Not exactly my cup of tea," she told Mike stoically.

"Why an invisible writer?" he asked her.

Sam looked at him blankly for a second, then realized that he'd gotten his terms confused. "You mean ghostwriter?"

He shrugged as he turned his key in the ignition again and drove back to the road. "Invisible, ghost, same thing," he told her glibly.

She supposed that in a way, it was. Besides, he didn't strike her as a man who liked to quibble over definitions while hunting for the appropriate word to describe something.

Sam addressed the gist of his question instead. "To answer your question, I like to write and more than that, I like to be able to delve into another person's life, find out what made that person who and what he or she was," she said honestly. "I like that they share their memories, their childhood, the special moments of their lives. Once I finish, I'm a part of them and they're a part of me. It gives me roots," she concluded.

He glanced in her direction. "Don't you have roots of your own?" he asked.

Maybe she'd said too much, Sam thought. But then, this cowboy probably really wasn't listening and what she said to him would be forgotten by morning. She risked nothing by sharing and maybe it would even do her some good, she speculated.

"Well, yes, sure," she acknowledged. "But they're very sparse roots. My father took off before I was born, so I never got to know him. For all I know, he was an orphan. My mother was hardly ever around, she was too busy earning a living and keeping the wolf from our door. And when she wasn't doing that, she was looking for Mr. Right."

"When she finally found him," Sam said glibly, "he was not only Mr. Right, but Mr. Right-Now. They got married and went off to parts unknown." The last time she'd seen her stepfather *or* her mother was at their wedding reception. It still hurt her to think about that, but she'd made the best of it.

"They just up and left you?" Mike asked incredulously. The look he spared her this time was longer and he appeared to be more interested than he had before.

Was that compassion she heard in his voice? The idea surprised her. He didn't strike her as someone who was capable of that sort of a reaction. Maybe she'd misjudged him.

At least she could hope so.

"Well, I wasn't exactly a baby in a basket that they sent drifting off to sea," she pointed out with a small, self-deprecating laugh. "I was eighteen and the truth of it was, I'd been on my own pretty much for years. My mother knew I could take care of myself." And then, of course, she added silently, there'd been Daniel. Daniel, whom she'd always been able to count on and lean on.

Until he wasn't there anymore and all she had to lean on was herself.

Mike had a feeling she was giving her mother far too much credit. He knew people like her mother. People whose vision was limited to what they saw in their bathroom mirror in the morning. Sam's mother undoubtedly had a sink-or-swim attitude toward her daughter when she threw her into the deep end of the emotional pool. In either outcome, whether it was sink or swim, the woman's hands were clean and she was free to just walk away from the responsibility for the human being she had brought into the world eighteen years ago.

Still, just because this woman sitting in his truck had had a hard time of it, that wasn't a reason he should feel sorry for her or treat her any differently than he treated most people he came across, Mike told himself.

But after a beat, without bothering to look in her direction, he recited the names of his siblings—in birth order. "Eli, Rafe, Gabe, Alma and Ray."

Talk about coming out of left field. Sam blinked, completely confused. "Excuse me?"

"You wanted names," he reminded her briskly. "Those are my brothers' and sister's names." Then, because she'd asked for more details, he gave her a little more to go on. "Eli has his own spread, Rafe is looking to have the same. Gabe and Alma work for the sheriff's office and Ray is still doing odd jobs around the ranch until he decides what to do with the rest of his life."

"How about you?" she asked. "Have you figured out what you want to do with 'the rest of your life'?"

He'd figured that out when he was five. "Run the main ranch," he told her simply.

In his opinion, as the oldest, there had never been any other course for him to take but that one. While it was true that the ranch officially belonged to all of them, someone had to handle the regular, day-to-day decisions that had to be made in order to keep it productive and running smoothly. Right now, that job belonged to his father, but more and more it was falling to him to be in the wings and ready to take over. He did it now for the short haul. Someday, that "haul" would be permanent. He neither resented it nor looked forward to it.

It was just the way it was.

It was his destiny.

Sam could tell by the cowboy's tone that he meant it. Apparently, he saw the ranch as his responsibility and despite his lack of effusive words, he obviously took that responsibility very seriously.

"No other hidden ambitions?" She couldn't help wondering.

"Nope," he answered with just the right amount of conviction to make the denial sound true. "I'm doing what I like. Or at least I will be once I get you delivered to the house," he amended.

She leaned forward to catch a glimpse of his face as she asked, "Didn't sign up to drive some woman from back East around, right?"

The shrug was neither dismissive nor self-conscious. "You said it, I didn't."

The man probably didn't realize that his body language gave away his thoughts. "You didn't have to. Everything about you says you resent being viewed as an errand boy—even if no one actually sees you that way," she added with emphasis. She certainly didn't.

"Just what would you know about it?" he asked.

His tone told her that she'd hit closer to home than he was happy about. She'd been studying people all her life. It had been one of her main interests as well as a source of diversion for as far back as she could remember. It cost nothing and brought an education with it.

"I know a little about having a chip on your shoulder," she countered kindly. "All it succeeds in doing is weigh you down and make you miserable. The sooner you get rid of it, the sooner you can see things in the right perspective."

Mike could feel his back going up. He didn't like being analyzed, even by an exceptionally attractive woman. "Looks like my father lucked out and got two for the price of one," he said sarcastically.

She didn't allow his tone to put her off. "I'm afraid I don't understand—"

"He got a ghostwriter *and* an armchair psychologist. Maybe even a lecturer thrown into the mix," he added for good measure.

Maybe she had that coming, Sam thought. She was usually better about keeping her opinions to herself. It was the silence that had gotten to her, made her talkative. Had he been a normal person, he would have felt uncomfortable about the silence as well and would have tried to get some sort of conversation going.

"Sorry, didn't mean to sound like I was lecturing— *or* psychoanalyzing you," Sam apologized. "I was just trying to tell you that I've been where you are and I know it's not a comfortable situation."

Mike turned his head and stared at her for a very long moment.

Granted it was October, but October in this region of Texas was not cold by any means. Still, she could have sworn she felt frost being sent in her direction.

"You mean like now?" he asked her.

Sam wasn't sure just what the cowboy was getting at, if he was being sarcastic again or if there was some sort of hidden meaning to his question. In any case, she had a feeling that any further discussion on the topic might lead to some sort of an argument and she did *not* want to begin her stay here with a confrontation with her client's son. That didn't bode well for what she hoped to accomplish here.

Winning an argument had never meant all that much to her.

Still, she really didn't just want to leave the subject hanging there either, so, in an effort to clarify things for herself, she ventured just one more question. "Did you try to talk your father out of hiring someone to work on your relative's journals for him?" She needed to know just how much he didn't want her here, although exactly *why* that was important wasn't crystal clear to her yet.

Mike shrugged. "I didn't know he was hiring someone until a few hours ago."

Maybe his resentment stemmed from being kept in the dark? That would explain his less than friendly attitude.

"You didn't know he'd hired anyone?" Sam asked.

Mike didn't know how much more clearly he could say it. "Not until he told me that he needed me to pick you up at the airport."

"That must have been some surprise." No wonder the man seemed so disgruntled. She wouldn't have been thrilled to have this sprung on her either.

Mike laughed then. It was a deep, robust laugh that sounded hearty rather than perfunctory. Sam found herself instantly captivated by the sound.

"I didn't know you had the gift of understatement," Mike said to her.

"I don't know if it's understatement so much as empathy," she corrected him, then confessed, "I can put myself into almost anyone's shoes. It's a bit confusing to be able to see both sides of an argument." At times it made her feel ambiguous, unable to back away from one side or the other. "But that does keep me fair," she added.

"And that's important to you?" he asked. He congratulated himself that not a shred of curiosity was discernible in his voice—even though he was.

"That is *very* important to me," she told him with emphasis. "Being unfair puts us on the same level as soulless creatures who are looking to get the better of anyone remotely threatening."

Before he could venture a comment, he saw the ranch house coming into view. They'd been on Rodriguez property for a bit now. That was when he realized that they had been traveling for close to an hour.

He supposed he had to grudgingly admit—if only to himself—that the constant droning of a conversation in the background made the time go by faster.

"We're here," he announced for her benefit as the ranch house grew steadily closer.

It was obviously the right thing to say—because Sam abruptly stopped talking.

Chapter Four

Sam took a deep breath before exiting the truck. It was her way of attempting to fortify herself before plunging into her surroundings and meeting the man who was responsible for her coming all the way out here from the East Coast.

The same excitement, as well as anxiety, that she always experienced before beginning a project danced through her. She both looked forward to this moment in a project and dreaded it. Dreaded it because there was always that part of her that worried she might be unequal to the job, that she would produce an uninspired work. It hadn't happened yet, but there was always a first time.

The excitement arose from the fact that at this moment in a project, she was standing on the threshold of endless possibilities, not the least of which was uncovering a world she'd never seen before.

Mentally crossing her fingers, Sam unbuckled her seat belt and slid out of the passenger seat. She'd worn her best outfit in hopes of creating a good impression and looking professional. Consequently, she had on high heels rather than the boots she realized would have been better for the dirt path that led from where Mike had stopped the truck to the three-storied, sprawling ranch house.

Just as Mike had pulled up to the house, Sam saw the front door open and a slightly heavyset, distinguished-looking older man came out onto the porch. Rather than stand there like a sentry, the man came down the three steps to her level. Far from solemn-looking, his smile was wide and inviting. In most situations she was the perpetual outsider, but here Sam felt instantly at home.

Miguel Rodriguez Sr. had that sort of quality about him.

And if his very presence didn't do it, the expression on his rounded face, coupled with a genuine embrace, conveyed that friendliness to any visitor who stepped onto his property.

"Welcome to my home," he declared from the midst of a bear hug. Releasing Sam, he stepped back and told her, "Thank you for coming."

"I should be thanking *you* for hiring me," Sam countered. "Most of my clients don't hire me until after they've asked to see a sample of my work and a list of all the projects I've worked on." She looked at the man with genuine wonder. "You didn't."

"Olivia Santiago gave me your name," Miguel told her simply. "She said you were a friend of a friend who worked with you and they were very pleased with what you did. That was more than good enough for me," he admitted honestly.

She'd never been confronted with such blatant trust before. The world she came from held people suspect until proven otherwise.

"I'll try not to disappoint you," she told him sincerely.

"I am sure that you will not," he told her with conviction. Glancing over her shoulder, he saw Mike taking out her suitcase and the briefcase containing her laptop. When nothing else followed, Miguel eyed his houseguest curiously. "Are the rest of your things being shipped out?"

"There is no 'rest of her things,'" Mike told his father before she could.

Miguel looked quizzically from his son to his guest. "You're not staying long?" he asked.

"I'm staying as long as it takes," she assured him. Then, to make things clearer, she told her new teddy-bear of an employer, "I don't need much."

"Ah, a lady after my own heart." He patted her hand before slipping it through the crook of his arm. "We will get along just fine," he predicted.

If she wasn't inclined to do the very best job she could each and every time she undertook a new assignment, Miguel would have made her want to reach that pinnacle now. He definitely had a winning way about him, she thought. And he was certainly a great deal friendlier and more welcoming than his oldest son was.

"How was your trip?" Miguel asked as he led her up the porch steps and into the house.

"Uneventful," she replied.

For a moment, he considered her words, then realized that perhaps she had misunderstood his question. "I am asking about your trip from the airport to the ranch with my son." He glanced toward his son. "He does not talk much, but all the others were busy, so I had no choice," Miguel explained. "Still, his heart is in the right place."

"Slightly left of center, where it's always been, Dad," Mike said with a touch of impatience. He was thirty-one and had been a man for a long time now. He didn't appreciate being discussed as if he was eleven, clueless and out of earshot.

With a less than pleased grunt, Mike picked up the two pieces of their houseguest's luggage and made his way into the house behind his father and Sam. "She staying in Alma's old room?" he asked so he could drop off her things in the right room.

Miguel nodded, then explained to Sam, "Alma is my daughter."

"The deputy," Sam acknowledged.

"You know Alma?" Miguel asked, surprised that the young woman was acquainted with his daughter.

"No—" she was quick to set the record straight "—I asked Mike about his siblings and he told all their names and what they did for a living."

Now that *really* surprised the older man. "You got him to talk? I am impressed."

"Still here, Dad," Mike reminded his father, doing his best to curb his exasperation.

There was no point in losing his temper. He knew what his father was like and there was no changing the man at this stage of the game any more than he could hope to change the spots on a leopard.

"So I see," Miguel acknowledged. He closed the front door behind his son, then instructed him, "Show Miss Monroe—"

Sam was quick to interrupt. "Call me Sam, please," she urged.

Miguel smiled warmly at the petite young woman. He'd already taken measure of her and he liked what he saw. As did, he suspected, his son. Miguel, Jr. just needed a little prodding and he was more than ready to do that. By his reckoning, he had approximately six weeks to make that happen.

"Show Sam to her room, please, Miguel," he requested. "And when you are settled in," Miguel continued, addressing his words to Sam, "we will talk and get acquainted." His eyes crinkled as he added, "I am looking forward to that."

Sam was anxious to get started as soon as possible, to sink her teeth into the project and immerse herself in a brand-new world that was significantly different from her own.

But she knew Miguel was right. There were steps to follow. She didn't want him to think he had brought a fanatical workaholic into his house even though that was probably the best description of her.

"I'll be down very soon," she promised for form's sake as she hurried to follow Mike.

The latter hadn't stopped to allow her to catch up. Instead, he'd already disappeared by the time she was halfway up the stairs.

Moving faster, Sam reached the landing just as she saw him walking into a room on the far right-hand side.

No coddling from that quarter, which was fine as far as she was concerned. She didn't expect to be coddled and wouldn't have really known how to react if she had been. It was foreign to everything she had experienced up to this point. The people she'd worked with prior to this assignment had all been forthcoming, but there had never been any pampering and she preferred it that way.

The cowboy certainly had some stride, she thought just as she reached the room that he'd entered. The second she did, her mind went blank.

Sam all but froze in the doorway, looking around the nine-by-twelve room. The bedroom appeared to be as welcoming as the man downstairs had been.

It was obviously a girl's room, yet it wasn't given over to frills and "girly" things. An individual had lived and slept here, Sam decided as she looked around. And it looked as if that person would come walking back in at any moment.

There was no sign of dust in the room and it appeared to be well taken care of.

Recently.

"You sure your sister won't mind me staying in her room?" Sam asked her all-but-silent guide.

"Not unless she's decided to leave Cash and needs a place to stay," he answered glibly. "Until then, Dad says you can stick around."

"Cash?" Sam repeated. "Is that her husband?" she asked.

"Yeah," Mike confirmed in a monotone. His assignment completed, Mike turned to leave the room. There was only one problem with that. Their houseguest was still standing in the doorway, blocking his exit. Mike eyed her. "Unless you want me to get really familiar with you, Sam—" he deliberately underscored her name "—I can't leave with you standing there." He punctuated his statement with a long, expectant stare.

"Oh, sorry," she murmured, suddenly realizing

that she was blocking the way out. Sam moved to the side, giving him space, and thought she heard Mike mumble, "Thanks," but then it just might have been her imagination.

She chalked up the other thing to her imagination, as well. Specifically the way her pulse jumped when Mike wound up accidentally brushing against her as he exited the room. Sam had stepped to the side to give him what she thought was a sufficient amount of space to pass, but obviously she'd miscalculated.

It had been the most innocent and minute of contacts between two people, yet for just a moment, she felt like she'd touched a live wire. It had sent a very real, very powerful jolt through her system.

She was just wired in general, Sam silently argued. That was all. Anxious to begin, anticipating what was involved, nervous that she might not deliver well enough to please that really nice man downstairs.

Because Miguel *was* so nice, she was more determined than usual to deliver the goods and make sure that there were no regrets about hiring her.

That, she silently insisted, was the *only* reason she felt that odd sort of tingling sensation zigzagging throughout her body. After all, it wasn't as if she and Mike had had full-on body contact or anything of that nature.

It was all in her head, nothing more.

She could *still* feel that unexpected jolt echo through her body, damn it.

Breathe, Sam, breathe, she ordered herself. *And for heaven's sake, calm down. You don't want to lose this job before you begin.*

"Come down whenever you're ready," she heard

Mike tell her in a voice that he might have used to inform her that the weatherman predicted no change for the next month.

Thank goodness his father was friendlier, she thought. Otherwise, this could have turned out to be a very uncomfortable assignment. Or at least any further interaction with her employer might have been uncomfortable.

But for the most part, her work was done at a desk in a room removed from the daily interactions of the people living around her. So, uncomfortable or not, it really shouldn't have mattered all that much to her.

Her thoughts seemed to be colliding with one another in a haphazard way. What was the matter with her?

Maybe the trip out here had tired her out, Sam decided. The more she thought about it, the more of a viable possibility it became. Especially since she felt a little off her game.

That would change soon enough, after a good night's sleep, she promised herself.

Sam had barely closed the door and had time to place her suitcase on the bed, preparing to unpack, when she heard a quick, staccato rap on the bedroom door. As she turned toward it, ready to open the door herself, she was surprised to see it open on its own.

She didn't even get a chance to ask who it was.

A tall, strapping cowboy with a pretty face that echoed some of Mike's features came striding into the room even as he said, "What're you doing here before your shift's up?"

The question had no sooner come tumbling from the man's lips than he stared at her, as surprised to see her as she was to have the room serving as her bedroom invaded.

"You're not my sister," the cowboy declared.

"Not that I know of," Sam readily agreed with a grin. This had to be the youngest brother.

The man instantly backtracked as he began to assess the blonde in the bedroom.

"Hey, I'm sorry. I thought you were Alma, but you're not. I'm Ray, by the way." Still smiling, he furrowed his brow a little in confusion. It was a look known to make a woman's knees grow weak. And then fantasy took a backseat to reality. "Who are you?"

"I'm Samantha Monroe," she replied, taking a couple of small steps toward him as she extended her hand. "Sam to my friends."

"Well, Sam-to-your-friends, you wouldn't be a friend of Mike's, would you?" he asked uncertainly.

Sam laughed as she shook her head. "No, I sincerely doubt that your brother would ever categorize me as being that."

"But you do know Mike?" Ray asked, apparently trying to get his facts straight.

"Yes, I do," she told him. "Your brother brought me out here from the airport. I'm going to be working for your father," she began to explain.

"Whatever Dad has you doing, just tell me where I can sign up?" he asked with an enthusiasm Sam found both disarming as well as extremely sweet.

Nevertheless, the man needed to have his facts straightened out.

"I don't think you quite understand," she told the youngest of the Rodriguez brothers.

"There's no 'think' about it, Sam. My little brother gets his exercise jumping to conclusions," Mike told her, coming into the room. The expression on his face was stern as he turned toward his brother. "She's working for Dad, Ray, she's not here to entertain you."

Mike had been drawn by the voices and, knowing Ray's penchant for seducing pretty girls, he'd come to see if the woman his father had hired needed any saving from his brother.

She appeared to be holding her own, but knowing Ray, it was just a matter of time before his youngest brother wore away her resistance.

His assignment for the next six weeks or so was to keep his youngest brother at least an arm's length away from Sam—at all times. Otherwise, he had a feeling that it was going to take a lot longer for her to write this book.

Ordinarily, he would have found such an assignment annoying. That he didn't was troubling to Mike on its own.

Chapter Five

Ray laughed in response to his brother's comment about the woman in Alma's room not being there for his personal entertainment.

He didn't know about Mike, but by his standards, this woman was exceptionally attractive and he wouldn't have minded getting something going with her, but he had a feeling that definitely didn't have a chance in hell of happening if she saw him as some sort of a womanizer or insensitive jerk, which would have been the logical conclusion after hearing Mike's comment.

So he coupled his dismissive laugh with a denial. "You make it sound like I'm some kind of a Neander-thal, Mike." He was about to add that he was nothing of the kind, but he never got the chance.

"No, you're worse," Mike replied in an even voice that came across stripped of all emotion.

Both Ray and Sam looked at him, obviously waiting for him to elaborate, but he just left his sentence hanging in the air without any further embellishment on his part. In his experience, the attempt to articulate himself could be far more damaging.

"Why don't you go and tell Dad his guest'll be

down shortly?" It really wasn't so much a request or a suggestion as a barely veiled order for Ray to leave the room.

For his part, Ray was usually as easygoing as his brother was not, but he didn't care to be ordered around like a lackey, especially not in front of an attractive woman. It wasn't that this was some sort of a competition. Mike wasn't acting this way to impress the woman. His brother just didn't think like that. However, that was how it might look to his father's guest and Ray didn't take kindly to being belittled by anyone, not even by his oldest brother.

There was a wave of momentary unspoken tension in the air. Sam could sense it and the very last thing she wanted was to cause discord that could be traced back to her as its source. She was here strictly to work, not to cause trouble.

Since she didn't have a myriad of items to unpack and put away, she could always take care of that minor detail later. That was part of the beauty of traveling light. She wasn't faced with a preponderance of possessions to house or keep track of.

This lack of goods now allowed her to announce, "Why don't we all go down?" She flashed a cooperative smile at Mike. "I'm ready now."

He frowned and indicated the suitcase on her bed. "Don't you have to unpack?"

"My things aren't going anywhere and it only takes a few minutes to put everything I brought away," she told him, already moving toward the doorway. He blocked her access to the hallway. His broad shoulders alone seemed to fill the space up rather well. "Now you're in my way," she commented, referring to what he'd said to her a few minutes ago.

"Yeah, so I am," he murmured, taking a step back into the hall.

Mike noticed as she swept past him toward the stairs that there was just the slightest whiff of a stirring fragrance that made him think of honeysuckle blossoms in the spring.

Had to be some kind of perfume or cologne, he thought.

Ordinarily, he didn't care to have the air around him tainted with heavy, artificial scents, but what he'd just breathed in didn't fall under that category.

If he didn't know any better, he would have said the soft fragrance was even arousing.

Except that he didn't react that way. He kept tight control over himself at all times so that nothing could affect him.

Mike took in another deep breath, thinking to clear his head. Instead, he experienced the same sort of reaction as he had with the first breath.

Except that this time, he thought he'd felt his pulse jump, as well.

As if reading his mind, Ray whispered, "Smells pretty, doesn't she?" He punctuated his question with a wide grin that seemed almost knowing.

Mike didn't bother acknowledging the comment, and just strode past his brother.

MIGUEL TURNED FROM the fireplace when he heard the sound of footsteps on the tile directly behind him in the living room. He'd expected to see Sam and his oldest son coming down again. He was surprised to see Ramon accompanying them. Miguel hadn't realized that his youngest had come home just now. As far as he knew, Ramon was supposed to be working with the wranglers who were training the new horses.

"I see you have met my youngest," he said to Sam. His dark eyes shifted toward the son under discussion. "I hope you behaved yourself, Ramon." There was just the slightest touch of sternness in his voice.

If there was, Ray didn't acknowledge it. "I'm always a gentleman, Dad. I wouldn't know how to be anything else," he assured his father.

Ray's words were met with an amused snort that Mike didn't bother trying to disguise or hide. While he was certain that Ray never did anything that a woman didn't want, his brother had the guile and the ability to make that woman want to do all sorts of things.

Sam turned around and looked at him with eyes that seemed just a little too wide, a little too blue—and, Mike was beginning to discover, just a little too disturbing for him to take in stride.

So he did what he always did when confronted with a situation he didn't care for or want to deal with. He withdrew.

"If you won't be needing me anymore," he said to his father, already backing out of the room, "I've got things I need to take care—"

He didn't get a chance to finish his sentence. "Actually," Miguel said as he held up his hand, stopping his oldest son in his tracks as well as midsentence, "I do need you, Miguel." The patriarch's warm dark eyes shifted appreciatively to his houseguest. "I think that if Samantha is going to be staying with us for a while, she should be shown around Forever so that she can come and go comfortably without feeling like a stranger." Miguel turned back to Mike. "I'd like you to take her to town, show her where the general store is, the diner, the post office, any place you think she might need to see. You can also introduce her to the sheriff, to the doctor, and of course, to Miss Joan," the older rancher specified.

"Miss Joan?" Sam asked. She'd heard the slight inflection when Miguel had said the woman's name and she couldn't help wondering just where the woman fit into the whole scheme of this town.

Ray was quick to come through with an explanation for her. "Miss Joan runs the diner and she kind of runs the town, too. Nothing happens in Forever that she don't know about."

"*Does not* know about," Miguel corrected his son softly.

Though English hadn't been his first language, since it was the language of his adopted country, Miguel took great pains to speak it correctly. This dedication included not allowing any of his children to become lazy when it came to things like grammar.

"My son could have stated it better, but the general thought is true. Nothing happens in this town without Miss Joan knowing about it. I am sure she would appreciate meeting you. You will find her to be a great source of the history of this region," Miguel told her.

Sam didn't need to hear anything further. She was hooked.

"I can take her into town," Ray volunteered, then tagged on with emphasis, "Since Mike's busy and everything."

But Miguel wasn't comfortable about turning over

this chore to his youngest. "He is not busy, are you, Miguel?" the older man asked, his dark eyes pinning his oldest the way no one else could.

Mike sighed and shoved his hands into his back pockets. Whatever plans he had he merely adjusted. Life had taught him how to be exceedingly flexible when it came to things like schedules.

"Guess not."

Since Mike's response was less than enthusiastic, Sam turned to her client, ready to beg off. "Mr. Rodriguez, I appreciate the thought, really, but I don't want to put anyone out on my account. I can certainly go on a tour of your town some other time."

"Hey, I just volunteered to take her," Ray pointed out, reminding the others. "There's no need to postpone anything."

"He's right," Mike spoke up, his deep voice rumbling through the momentary stillness. "No need to postpone anything." But instead of reinforcing his brother's offer, Mike said, "I'll take her."

Looking to avoid being the object of a verbal tug of war between the two brothers, Sam announced in no uncertain terms, "I'm perfectly capable of going into town by myself."

"Nobody is disputing that," Miguel told her kindly, "but I have something I need Ramon to do so Miguel will be your guide. When you return, Rosa will have dinner ready," he promised her.

Mike could see that she looked a little confused by the introduction of another name. Probably wondering if that was another member of the family he'd failed to mention, Mike guessed. "Rosa's Dad's housekeeper," he explained.

"Oh, and she does not keep your house as well and you do not eat what she cooks?" Miguel asked, amused by his son's choice of words.

"*Our* housekeeper," Mike amended, stifling a sigh.

It bothered him to refer to the woman as his housekeeper since the woman received both her salary and her instructions from his father. He made sure he took care of his own things. Had this been his ranch to run exclusively, he would have been making his own meals, as well. Granted he was nowhere the cook that Rosa was, but on the other hand, he had never poisoned anyone either.

Mike looked at Sam and said, "If you want that tour, we'd better get going."

Not waiting for her to respond one way or another, Mike headed toward the front door and out of the house.

Sam found herself having to hurry in his wake.

"You setting her up?" Ray asked his father the minute the door was shut.

In the past couple of years, he'd seen four of his siblings become engaged, then married and only one union had occurred without some sort of secretive prodding by his father. Eli had needed no prodding to give in to the inevitable and marry Kasey. But then, Eli had been in love with her since elementary school.

"I am not setting up anyone," Miguel protested innocently. "I am simply not entrusting a lamb to a coyote," his father responded, looking at his youngest significantly.

"You really think that she's any safer being sent off with a lone wolf for company?" Ray asked.

Mike might have been a loner, but an exceptionally honorable one, Miguel thought. And yet he wasn't about to argue the point with Ramon. His youngest saw the world in a completely different way than his oldest did.

"You have horses to work with," Miguel reminded him.

"And they'll probably give me straighter answers than I'm getting here," Ray mumbled.

As Ray left the house again, Miguel smiled to himself. Looking through the front window, he caught a glimpse of Miguel and Samantha in the distance. He had high hopes for that pair, he mused. It was a definite bonus on top of what he'd initially bargained for—someone good to turn his ancestor's diaries into a coherent book.

Miguel Rodriguez felt very fortunate indeed.

REACHING MIKE'S TRUCK, Sam paused by the passenger door. There was no sense in making the man feel as if she was an albatross around his neck.

"If you drive me into town and drop me off at the car rental agency, you're free to go back home or do whatever you want instead of being stuck as my tour guide. I can take it from there."

Mike slanted a look in her direction. "I really doubt that."

Opening the door on his side, he waited for her to get in on her side. Instead, she continued standing there. For some reason, he saw that she looked annoyed, as well. Now what?

"Look, I don't know what the women around here are like, but I've been finding my own way around now for a long time," she informed him, taking offense at his dismissive attitude.

And then he took the wind out of her sails by saying, "I'm sure you have."

She hadn't a clue what to make of this man. "But you just said that you 'doubted that.'" If that wasn't derogatory, she didn't know what was. "I don't get it."

"What I said was," he repeated, pointing out the difference, "that I doubted you could rent a car."

Was he saying that she didn't look trustworthy? Or that whoever was in charge of car rentals wouldn't accept a credit card? She should have taken more cash out of her account, she thought, upbraiding herself.

"And just why can't I rent a car?" Sam asked.

There was just a hint of amusement in his answer. "Because Forever doesn't have car rental agency."

"Oh."

Just how small a town was this? No car rental agency, no hotel; it sounded as if this town was stuck in the beginning of the last century. Fragments of thoughts went through her head, only to be discarded. And then she thought of something.

"Do you have a car mechanic?" she asked Mike suddenly.

"We have one of those," he answered in an easy cadence. Giving up waiting for her to get in, he got in on his side and began to buckle up, then spared her an expectant look.

With a sigh, Sam got in.

"Mick," Mike told her, picking up the thread of the conversation after several beats. "His name is Mick. Why?" he asked.

"Well, sometimes mechanics have a loaner car that

they can let a customer have while they're working on their car." It was a long shot, but at the moment, it seemed to be the only way she could think of to get her own mode of transportation.

Mike drove toward the main road, the one that took him straight into Forever. "The key words here are 'their car,'" he pointed out.

He didn't have to sound like he was lecturing her. She was only trying to help him.

The next moment, she was saying as much to him since subtlety was apparently wasted on a man like that. "I'm just trying to get you out of having to act as my personal tourist guide." Although she had to admit, if only to herself, that she wouldn't have minded spending time with him—if only she didn't feel as if he thought it was some sort of penance on his part.

She rolled another idea over in her head. "I guess you could just drop me off in town, then pick me up later and you can just tell your father you took care of the introductions."

He spared her a look that she couldn't begin to fathom. "Are you telling me to lie?"

No good deed went unpunished, she thought grudgingly. "No. I'm not telling you to lie, I'm trying to get you out of having to do something you don't want to do."

"Number one, I didn't *say* whether I wanted to do 'it' or not, so don't assume anything and number two—more importantly than number one—I don't lie. I told my father I would take you on a tour of Forever, so I'll take you on a tour of Forever."

Sam was still chewing on what he'd told her—or claimed. "You don't lie," she repeated.

Why was that so hard for her to accept? he wondered. "No," he replied stoically.

"Ever?" she prodded, leaning forward in her seat to get a better look at his face.

"What part of 'I don't lie' is unclear to you?" he asked. It was apparent that his supply of patience was seriously running low.

Sam blew out a breath. "No part," she freely admitted. It wasn't that she didn't understand what he was claiming, she just didn't know whether she actually believed him. "I just never met anyone who didn't, let's say, 'bend the truth' once in a while when it was to their advantage."

"Well, now you have." He gave her a penetrating look that was meant to intimidate her. That it failed both annoyed him and evoked in him a grudging respect for her feistiness. "Are you going to argue with me all the way into town, or are you finally going to stop looking a gift horse in the mouth and just accept the fact that you lucked out?" he asked.

A few choice, hot words rose to her lips, but she managed to keep them under wraps. Someday, though, she promised herself, she and this man were going to have it out—and she would put him in his place the way no one else apparently ever did.

"Did anyone ever tell you that you have a winning personality?" she asked him.

He kept his eyes on the road. "No, I don't believe anyone ever did."

She would have easily bet money on that outcome.

"Well, I don't think I'd hold my breath, waiting, if I were you."

"I don't foresee anyone running up alongside the truck in the next couple of minutes, so I won't."

It took effort not to stare at him with her mouth hanging open. "Do you take everything literally?" she asked.

He did and there was a reason for that. "Most people don't exaggerate around here."

She thought tall tales came with the territory. "This *is* Texas, isn't it?"

"Yes, why?"

Sam shut her eyes as she shook her head. "Never mind," she murmured, surrendering for the moment. The man probably had no imagination and no sense of humor, two things she'd always thought to be of vital importance in the composition of a human being.

It was going to be a very long trip into town and back, Sam thought.

She slanted a look in his direction. "So you and Ray are brothers, huh?" That had just slipped out, caused by her surprise that two brothers could be as different as night and day, the way that these two apparently seemed to be.

"So they tell me," Mike responded dryly. He fixed her with a quizzical look. "Why?"

Sam shrugged, doing her best to sound as disinterested in the conversation as she thought he was. But she couldn't pull it off. She was *always* interested in what people felt and had to say. "No reason, you just seem very different from one another."

They were and Mike was well aware of it. He and Ray had grown up under different circumstances.

"That's because Ray is the youngest and working hard seems more like a choice to him than a responsibility."

She had always been fascinated by people and their stories. Today was no exception—especially not after he'd just said that. "But it doesn't to you?" she asked.

"Nope."

His answer led her to another question. "Do you ever have fun, Mike?"

He glanced at her. "You mean that we're not having fun now?"

She stared at him, her hand splayed across her chest. "Dear God, was that an actual joke?"

Mike shrugged carelessly in response. "Far as I know, that was a question."

But she could have sworn she saw a glimmer of a smile on his lips. The corners of his mouth had curved just a little.

There was hope, she thought. The man just might actually have a sense of humor. And that heartened her immensely.

Chapter Six

The diner was doing a fair amount of business when she and Mike walked in through the door. Despite that, Sam could feel that she had instantly drawn the attention of the older woman behind the counter. Of average height and somewhat on the thin side, the woman had hair that was slightly too red and hazel eyes that gave the impression that they missed *nothing.*

Sam saw that her "guide" was making his way across the diner and directly to the woman. She had no choice but to follow.

This, Sam assumed, had to be the famous "Miss Joan."

The woman finished filling the customer's coffee cup and set the pot down. A wry smile curved Miss Joan's thin lips as she slowly looked her over. "You Rodriguez boys just keep attracting pretty women like bees to honey, don't you?"

Her words might have been addressed to Mike, but the woman was looking directly at her. Shy by nature though she struggled daily to overcome that tendency, Sam felt a strong urge to shift from foot to foot. She didn't do well being so closely scrutinized. It wasn't that she had anything to hide, but being examined so thoroughly, especially by a stranger, always made her feel as if she would come up lacking.

Since the woman had addressed him, Sam waited for Mike to make some sort of a response. But he merely made a noise that sounded suspiciously more like a grunt than something intelligible.

"It's not what you think," Mike finally told the woman.

The thin smile spread a little more. "How would you know *what* I was thinking, boy?"

Wisely choosing not to get drawn into that conversation, Mike merely told her, "She's here to work with my father."

If anything, that served to pique the older woman's curiosity rather than satisfy it. "Work with him?" the woman repeated, her eyes shifting from one to the other. "Work with him how?"

She didn't like being talked about as if she was an inanimate object. And, Sam supposed she wasn't telling any tales out of school if she answered the woman's question herself. After all, Miguel Rodriguez was the one who had thought having her orient herself with the town was a good idea. In her experience, people in small towns liked knowing all about anyone who entered their vicinity.

"Mr. Rodriguez hired me to go through his great-great-great-grandmother's diaries and journals. He wants to have them transcribed and put in chronological order so that they can be read as a detailed memoir," she explained. Then, not waiting any longer for an introduction, she offered her hand to the woman behind the counter. "Hi, I'm Samantha Monroe. You can call me Sam," she added, still struggling to keep from squirming beneath the woman's unwavering stare.

A moment passed before the woman made her decision. Sam assumed that she passed muster because the woman took her hand and shook it. "And you can call me Miss Joan," she told Sam. "Everyone does."

Sam forced herself to relax. She had a feeling she'd passed the first inspection. "Miss Joan," she repeated, doing her best to smile.

"Sit down, take a load off," Miss Joan urged, gesturing toward the stools lining the counter. "What's your pleasure? We've got tea to calm you down and coffee to rev you up." The woman glanced in Mike's direction. "Although I suspect that Mike can probably do the same thing."

Something inside Sam's stomach tightened in response, even as she told herself she had no idea what the woman was talking about.

"That's enough, Miss Joan," a woman's voice from behind Sam told the owner of the diner. "Don't go embarrassing the girl her first few minutes in your establishment."

Sam saw Miss Joan look over her head toward the woman who had just spoken. "Just because you're married to my stepson doesn't mean you can sass me, girl." The woman's voice was stern but it was impossible to know what her mood actually was.

"No," the woman agreed. "I can sass you because you know I'm right. The poor girl's got enough to deal with, just being shown around town by Mike. Hi," the vibrant dark-haired and very visibly pregnant young woman said to Sam, putting out her hand by way of a greeting. "I'm Alma, Mike's sister," she said, introducing herself.

"More like my cross to bear," Mike commented. Sam noticed that there wasn't so much as a hint of a smile on his face as he said that.

"Right back at you, big brother." Unconsciously resting her hand on the pronounced swell of her abdomen, Alma looked at the newcomer. Her voice dropped half an octave as she instructed, "Don't let my brother intimidate you."

"You mean his bark is worse than his bite?" Sam guessed.

"No, his bite's worse, but just don't let him intimidate you," she repeated. "Give him as good as he dishes out," she added. "The rest of us would love to see him put in his place."

Mike shot her a dark look, then laughed. "You should live so long," he told her.

Alma merely smiled at him. "That's my dream, big brother. So," Alma continued, switching her attention to the new face in the diner, "have you had a chance to look at the diaries Dad found?"

Sam shook her head. "Not yet, but I'm looking forward to it. Your father thought I should go on a tour of your town first, learn my way around," she explained as to what she was doing here instead of being on the ranch.

"Tiny, isn't it?" Alma asked with a laugh.

"Where are you from?" Miss Joan asked without any preamble, her very voice commanding attention from her.

Sam immediately turned toward the older woman. "I live in New York," she answered.

"Then this town must seem *really* tiny to you," Alma speculated.

Miss Joan, however, wasn't all that convinced she'd given the right answer. "Not with that accent you're not. Where're you from originally?" Miss Joan pressed.

Was it that obvious to the woman? Sam wondered. She'd worked hard to erase her initial accent. Her goal had always been to sound as if she could fit in anywhere, come from anywhere. No doubt, she couldn't fool this woman's ear.

"Originally, Broken Saber, Oklahoma. But we moved to Maryland when I was about three."

This answer the old woman found acceptable. "That's more like it," Miss Joan said with a triumphant nod of her head. "Knew there was another accent lurking around your words."

Alma glanced at her watch. "Well, I'd better be getting back. Miss Joan, you have the sheriff's coffee?" she asked.

"Fresh and ready to go," the woman replied, producing a tall covered container and puting it on the counter. In exchange, Alma placed a couple of bills on the counter before she picked up the coffee. Miss Joan frowned deeply, pushing the bills back toward the deputy. "Take that back, girl. The sheriff knows his money's no good here."

Alma made no effort to retrieve the bills. Instead, she deliberately ignored them even when Miss Joan moved them closer to her on the counter. "You know how he feels about that, Miss Joan."

Impatience fleetingly passed over her pale features.

Miss Joan took Alma's hand and pressed the bills into her palm.

"Tell him to come argue with me himself if it means that much to him," she told the sheriff's deputy. "Until then, not another word." It wasn't a request, it was an order.

Alma looked as if she was about to say something, but then thought better of it. Everyone knew that arguing with Miss Joan was nothing short of a colossal waste of time and effort.

"Don't people win arguments with Miss Joan?" Sam asked Mike in what she thought was a soft whisper.

Having made her way down the counter to wait on another customer, Miss Joan was still able to hear her. "Not hardly. Only one who ever did is Harry."

Sam looked to Mike for an explanation. "Harry?"

It was Miss Joan who answered. "My husband— and he only won because I wanted him to," she emphasized the point. Miss Joan looked over toward the sheriff's deputy who hadn't left the diner yet. "You might want to remind your boss of that little fact when you bring him that coffee—which, by the way, is going to start growing cold if you don't get a move on, girl." The hazel eyes deliberately shifted toward the door.

Alma turned to leave, uttering a friendly, "See you later," to Miss Joan.

The deputy's manner, Sam couldn't help thinking, was every bit as warm and outgoing as her father's. Sam had a hunch that the whole family had that sort of a personality—all except for Mike, it seemed. Had he been hiding behind some wall—or better yet, some cloud—when warmth was being handed out to his family?

Or was his lack of warmth because he had gotten an extra dose of good looks instead? Because there was no disputing the fact that of the four Rodriguez family members whom she had met so far, in her opinion Mike was the handsomest one.

Of course, Sam amended, she hadn't met the other three yet, but if any of the others were more handsome than Mike was, she reasoned that it would probably hurt just to look at him.

Okay, get a grip, Sam. You're here to work, not to drool or have extraneous thoughts that aren't directly connected to turning out the very best possible product that you possibly can.

"Nice meeting you," Alma called out to her as she started to leave. She lingered for another second to issue a good-natured warning to her older brother. "You be on your best behavior, you hear?" She pinned Mike with a significant look.

"You're forgetting who's the older one," Mike retorted, raising his voice as he called after his exiting sister. It was against his nature to be vocal around others, but he had no choice at the moment. And there was no way he wanted her to think he was cutting her any extra slack because of her condition. Alma would have had his head if she thought that.

"No, I'm not," was Alma's final say on the matter. His sister was gone before he could go on record with a rejoinder.

Miss Joan immediately turned her attention back to Miguel's houseguest.

"You been doing this long?" she asked. When Sam

looked at her uncertainly, the woman added, "Spending time putting down other people's words for them in your own fashion?"

That wasn't quite what she did, but Sam didn't want to get into the particulars right now. The diner owner might think she was challenging her. So instead, she said, "A few years."

Miss Joan nodded, absorbing the answer. "You any good at it?" she asked.

The woman certainly didn't waste time with niceties and beating around the bush, Sam thought. "I'd like to think so."

"Good," Miss Joan pronounced with a nod of her head. "You've got confidence." She smiled, then added, "Hang on to it." Picking up her ever-present coffeepot, the woman filled a cup with steaming black coffee, then slid both the creamer and the sugar over next to it.

Sam raised her eyes from the cup to look at Miss Joan. "I didn't order anything," she protested.

"No, I did," the woman told her. "I thought it might help you hold your own against this one." To underscore her point, Miss Joan inclined her head in Mike's direction. "He'll roll right over you if you give him half a chance," she warned.

"And coffee is supposed to help stop him?" Sam asked skeptically.

"Well, it sure can't hurt," Miss Joan countered.

"What about me?" Mike asked the feisty woman he had known all his life.

Miss Joan regarded him with barely veiled amusement. "What about you, handsome?"

"Don't I get a coffee?" he asked.

Miss Joan laughed. "You, handsome, are revved up enough as it is. And no amount of tea in the world is going to counteract that. I'm just trying to level the playing field for this little lady." About to carry away the coffeepot, Miss Joan paused and patted Sam's hand. "You got any questions, honey, you find your way back to me."

"What kind of questions?" Sam asked. Was the woman talking about questions regarding the history of the countryside, or was she alluding to something a little more personal?

Miss Joan's hazel eyes danced with humor as she leaned in toward her. "*Any* kind of questions," she emphasized. The next moment, the woman was working her way down the counter, calling out a greeting to two men who had just walked into the diner and taken seats on the far end.

Sam could feel Mike looking at her. The next minute, he asked her, "Ready to go?"

The way she saw it, she was fitting into *his* schedule so it was up to him to determine when they left. "You're the guide," she pointed out.

"Doesn't mean I'm going to be dragging you around from place to place when you're not ready to leave. Now, you ready or not?" he asked.

Sam drained her cup and set it back down on the saucer, feeling a definite jolt to her system as the coffee wound its way throughout her body.

"Ready," she declared.

Sam found herself saying the word to his back. Mike was already on his feet, heading for the door. He might not have any intentions of dragging her around, but neither, apparently, did he intend to hang around and wait for her, either.

Figuring the man out was going to take a lot of patience on her part, Sam decided.

She had just enough time to slide off her stool, wave goodbye to Miss Joan and hurry after the man. He was, after all, her ride back.

Well, one good thing, Sam thought in her never-ending quest to find the positive side of every situation. She certainly wasn't going to be lacking for exercise on this assignment.

RATHER THAN WHISK her back to the ranch, the way she expected, Mike told her that he was taking her to all the places that his father would want her to see. He also made it known that he thought this tour was rather pointless. Since she had no car of her own, if she had any desire to go to town for some reason, she'd have to ask one of them to take her, hence negating any need for her to learn her way around Forever and the roads that led to it.

But Mike knew better than to point out the obvious to his father. Miguel Rodriguez marched to a different drummer than he did, but since he was his father— and he did love the old man—Mike gave him the respect that was his due.

Secretly, Mike had to admit that he was rather curious to see how a New Yorker would react to their less-than-sophisticated little blip on the map. Granted she had mentioned something about originally coming from Oklahoma, but the last place she'd lived would be the most vivid to her.

Forever didn't exactly fare well in a comparison to New York City.

"You had enough?" Mike asked her abruptly as they left the sheriff's office.

"You make it sound like an endurance test," she told him.

"Isn't it? For you?" he added in case she thought that was his take on the town. This was where he'd been born and raised and he had no regrets if this was also going to be the place where he died. Everything he wanted was right here within the town limits or on the ranch.

Sam abruptly stopped walking. She'd promised herself to just go with the flow, not challenge the man or take offense at his edgy, critical manner. But she was going to be living at the ranch and despite what she foresaw as a dedicated work schedule, their paths were destined to cross every so often.

She wanted the air cleared now rather than to have a future confrontation hanging over her head. Hands on her hips, she faced him. "Why are you so angry at me?"

He barely spared her a look as he strode past. "I'm not angry."

But Sam wasn't going to be ignored. She grabbed his arm—or rather, his sleeve, and said, "Trust me, on my end of this, you definitely sound angry. Why?"

"Because I think this is a waste of time."

She tried to untangle his meaning. "A waste of time taking me around, or a waste of time, my transcribing the journals?"

His eyes all but pinned her in place. "Yes," he answered. The next moment, he'd shaken her hand off and was heading for his truck.

"Well, that certainly cleared things up," she said sarcastically. Sam was fairly trotting now to keep up, but she would have rather died than asked the man to slow down. "It's me you object to, isn't it?"

It wasn't her he objected to, it was the money. They were doing well now, but it wasn't all that long ago that foreclosure was a reality. He didn't want it making a reappearance and the best way he knew how to avoid that was by keeping spending down to a minimum.

"Don't see why he needed to bring someone in just to read a bunch of books and pull out the highlights. Any one of us could do that for him," Mike informed her coldly.

It was beginning to make more sense now, she supposed, although she didn't appreciate his passing judgment on the quality of her work before she had a chance to even produce it.

"And you told him this?" She assumed his answer was yes.

But he surprised her by saying, "No."

They reached the truck. Tired of talking to the back of his head, she moved quickly to get in front of him and was all but in his face as she asked her next question. "But you're willing to spend the time doing it for him."

The shrug was impatient as well as frustrated. "Not exactly now, but soon."

Triumph blossomed on her face. For a moment, it mesmerized him—until he forced himself to dismiss both her face and the emotion she was radiating.

"That's the whole point," Sam insisted, not about to

be summarily rejected. "'Soon' doesn't come nearly as quickly as promised—if at all. Bringing someone like me into the project just makes it a reality instead of a wish."

The expression on his face announced that he was already bored with the topic and he shrugged his shoulders, muttering, "Whatever you say." But for once he didn't say it nearly as grudgingly or dismissively as she'd expected.

Sam read between the lines and realized that she had a minuscule chance to make a true believer out of a skeptic.

She fully intended to.

That became her real challenge rather than the project she'd agreed to take on. She knew she was capable of handling this project. Oh, there might be a couple of false starts along the way, but at this point in her work, she knew she could more than do it justice.

It was the former—making Mike into a believer, not just of her but of the entire process, of the need for people to connect across the generations—that would prove to be a test of her abilities.

Sam told herself that she was up to it.

Now all that remained was to make sure she hadn't bitten off more than she could chew.

Chapter Seven

"When you were growing up, did your brothers or sister sometimes tag along after you when you were hanging out with your friends?" Sam asked him.

The question seemed to come out of the blue. It took him a few seconds to process it. "I didn't do a lot of 'hanging out' when I was growing up," Mike informed her coolly.

There was always something to do on the ranch, horses to feed, stalls to clean out, along with the normal load of schoolwork. Attending to each didn't exactly leave all that much time for him to be young and irresponsible, which was what "hanging out with friends" meant to him.

"But you did do it once in a while, right?" Sam persisted.

He shrugged. "Maybe." Where was all this going? And why was this so important to her? "What's your point?" he asked.

"My point," Sam told him, lengthening her stride for the umpteenth time in order to keep up with him as they walked through Forever, "is that if one of your brothers or sister *did* tag along after you against your expressed wishes, I'm guessing that this had to be what they felt like."

He stopped walking to regard her in earnest. Since he did it without warning, Sam bumped right into him. He caught her by the shoulders to steady her. It was either that, or he would be forced to pick her up off the ground. This seemed the better way to go, even if it did involve touching her—and experiencing an unsettling reaction to the contact despite his attempt to merely dismiss it.

"What the hell are you talking about?" he asked.

It took Sam a second to get her bearings. He was still holding her by the shoulders, still causing her startled insides to scramble and knot and her heart to rev up and race unaccountably.

She forced herself to keep her mind on the conversation and not some random, unspoken cluster of sensations, no matter how much they made her insides quicken.

"I'm talking about feeling like a burden, like someone trying to keep up with a person who would really be happier if I was still somewhere on the other side of the country. Look, I meant it when I told you that you didn't have to show me around. I'm used to getting around on my own. It's not as if this were something new for me."

"And I told you that I told my father I would do it and I'm as good as my word, so there's no point in debating this. If you don't like the way I'm handling this little tour, then *you're* free to go back to the ranch. Just say the word and I'll take you."

"Oh, no, I'm not going to be the one to throw in

the towel." She squared her shoulders. "Okay, what else is on the agenda?"

So far, Mike had taken her to the emporium and introduced her to the couple who ran the store, had pointed out the movie theater that only opened after sundown during the week and had taken her by the medical clinic run by the town's only doctor who, coincidentally, was married to the sheriff's sister-in-law. He took her by the saloon, Murphy's, the only place in town where alcohol was sold, and rounded out her tour by bringing her to the sheriff's office, where she ran into Alma again as well as met the sheriff and the two other deputies—Mike's brother Gabe and Joe Lone Wolf, a full-blooded Navajo Indian. The latter had asked her if she'd had a chance to see the reservation yet.

At the mention of a reservation in the area, Sam's eyes had widened and she'd answered that she hadn't even known there *was* a reservation in the area. At that point, Mike announced they had to be going, thereby abruptly cutting the conversation short and, incidentally, prompting Sam's question about being regarded as a tagalong as they left the sheriff's office.

Mike made no effort to stifle the impatient sigh he exhaled. None of this had been easy for him. While he did like the people who lived and worked in Forever, bringing Sam around and making all those introductions wasn't exactly a piece of cake—or second nature for him. On his own, he tended to keep to himself. If he averaged ten words an hour, he considered that talkative.

"This is about the reservation, isn't it?" he asked her.

"In part," she allowed. She did want to go see it,

but he didn't seem inclined to go anywhere else today. "But it's also about feeling as if I'm a burden to you."

"Well, you are," he said bluntly, the retort just coming out on its own. The next moment, he reconsidered his answer when he saw the look on her face. She was trying to mask it, but he could see that he'd hurt her feelings.

Well, what did he expect? he upbraided himself. After all Sam *was* a female and even Alma didn't have a hide like a rhino all the time—just most of it.

He tried his hand at a little damage control and attempted to backtrack. "But I guess that's not your fault," he said expansively in an attempt to erase the sting of his previous words. At a loss how to make this better, he threw up his hands. "Look, I'm not a people person."

"I would have never guessed." But there was an amused smile on her lips so he decided she didn't mean that sarcastically.

"Maybe you would have been better off if Ray had been the one to take you around," he told her. "Ray's a people person. He's better at this kind of stuff— introductions and small talk—and I can probably train those horses better than he can."

"I'm sure you probably could." He struck her as the kind of man who could do anything he set his mind to without any limits, although she hadn't a shred of evidence to back up her beliefs. She was just going entirely on her gut. "But I'm not complaining," she pointed out.

"Then what was that bit about feeling like a kid brother tagging along?" He wanted that cleared up.

Was she just making a wisecrack, or was there something behind her comparison?

"That was a statement of fact," she informed him. "You were treating me exactly like some kid you were hoping to lose in the crowd and I thought that maybe you weren't aware of it and if I brought the matter to your attention—"

"I'd stop doing it," he concluded.

Sam inclined her head, indicating he'd guessed it on the first try. "Something like that."

And then Sam searched his face, wondering if she'd crossed a line and offended him. For a moment she thought she had, but then he asked her, "You want to see the reservation?"

Well, she wasn't expecting that. He certainly knew how to catch a person off her guard.

"I'd love to," she told him with enthusiasm.

"It's not going to be like the Hollywood version of an outdoor flea market or whatever it is that they call these things in places where people can't make ends meet from week to week on what they can raise," he told her, then informed her gruffly, "You're not going to see colorful blankets spread out on the ground with all sorts of jewelry, clothes and moccasins on them, made by some enterprising Navajo who's trying to sell them."

"I'm not expecting that," she told him sincerely. Taking a breath, she asked, "Just how run-down is the reservation?"

Her question surprised him. Maybe she wasn't as naive as he thought. "It's better now than it used to be," he answered. "Joe and Ramona got the younger tribe members to take some pride in their homes and since then, things are steadily being built up. Still got a long ways to go, but at least they've gotten started."

That was what she wanted to see. The places where progress was being made. In addition, she really wanted to be able to connect to the locals since their ancestors had probably been the ones who had captured Miguel's ancestor all those many years ago. She wanted to be able to see what Marguerite had seen, view it through her eyes.

"You mentioned someone named Ramona," Sam began to ask.

"That's the sheriff's sister—Joe's wife," he told her as they headed back to his truck. "She's also the local vet. Both Rick and Ramona have some Navajo blood in them, as well as a mixture of other tribes," was all he'd say on the subject. As far as he was concerned, announcing their heritage or keeping it private was up to Rick and his sister, not him.

"I guess that makes them all-American," Sam theorized.

"Yeah, I guess it does."

Maybe taking this woman around wasn't really so bad after all, Mike grudgingly thought. And, except for the reservation, which he saw to be more or less of a drive-by, they were done. That meant he would have several hours of good daylight left. He could still get a few things done once they got back to the ranch— if the woman didn't ask too many questions and hold him up, Mike silently qualified.

THE ALL-TOO-QUICK drive through the Navajo reservation had left her extremely quiet. He didn't think it was natural, not for her.

Mike glanced at her to see if she'd fallen asleep. But her eyes were open. As for her expression, she seemed to look solemn.

"Something wrong?" he finally asked, thinking that if there *was* something wrong, he'd do better to find out now instead of later, when he got her back to the ranch house. He'd gotten to know her well enough today to feel that having her so quiet—especially voluntarily—was almost eerie.

"That's better?" Sam finally asked him.

Sam's question caught him completely off guard. "What?"

"You said that the conditions on the reservation have improved," she reminded him, banking down her impatience. "I asked if what I saw represented 'better' in your estimation."

Was that all? "Well, it's not going to make the front page of any magazine, but yeah, what you saw today is actually better. Remember, I said better than it used to be," he qualified.

"Yes, you did say that," she agreed, backing off and willing to give him the benefit of the doubt. But she was still left wondering how people could accept living in those conditions. A lot of the homes she saw were little more than shells constructed against the elements. "Is there anything I can do?"

He wasn't following her. "About what?"

"About the conditions on the reservation," she stressed, enunciating each word slowly and with emphasis. "Some of those homes looked like they didn't even have any electricity." She tried to imagine what it had to be like, doing without power, without lights—

and couldn't fathom it lasting for more than an hour or two.

"Some of them don't," he informed her with a shrug. That was just the way things were. "But as far as *you* doing something about the conditions, well, that's a tricky road to walk." After all, she wasn't one of them and they did take offense easily. "The people on the reservation have got a hell of a lot of pride. They don't like being in someone's debt—and they sure as hell don't like being thought of as charity cases."

That wasn't how she saw them, but she had a feeling that saying so wasn't the solution. "Well, I wouldn't want to insult them," she told him.

The wheels in her head were spinning. She had some connections through her work. The book that she'd done two books before this one had been for a man, Andrew Whitman, who had built himself up. He'd gone from nothing to owning too many corporations to count. Wanting to give back, he was always looking for worthwhile causes. She could give him a call, tell him about the reservation.

"I was just thinking along the lines of a fundraiser," she told Mike, the eagerness in her voice growing.

"Still charity," Mike pointed out.

"There are kids involved," she countered. She'd seen several groups of children with eyes mirroring souls that were far older that the bodies that housed them.

"Pride should take a backseat when it comes to taking care of children. Besides, I'm not talking about some sort of endless charity, I'm talking about a helping hand, something to get them kick-started. You know, teach a man to fish rather than give a man a fish kind of a thing."

Mike supposed that the woman meant well. She certainly didn't look like one of those people who enjoyed building up their own self-esteem by slumming about in areas that were badly in need of help, coming up with suggestions that were engineered, for the most part, to make themselves look better and little else.

"Run whatever idea you have past Joe," he suggested. "He'd be the one who could tell you if what you were proposing was going to work or not." And then a thought suddenly hit him. "Does this mean you're not going to be working on those journals my dad found?"

Was that hope she heard in his voice? She really couldn't tell. The man certainly played his cards close to his vest.

"No, that's still my first priority," she told him in no uncertain terms. "It's just that seeing the reservation kind of made everything more vivid for me."

Mike nodded at her words in such a way she felt as if they had just gone in one ear and out the other. And then he asked her, "You about ready to start heading back to the house?"

She was rather tired—all in all, with the trip, plus the tour, she had put in an extremely long day—and it wasn't nearly over yet. Sam nodded in response to his question. "I think that I've seen enough for one day. Thanks," she added in a whole different tone.

The single word, enthusiastically uttered, threw him. "For what?"

She smiled at him. "For being my guide, however reluctantly."

There was no point in attempting to correct her. He *had* started out reluctantly, feeling more like an unpaid nanny than a guide or anything else. But this tour that had been forced on him had also allowed him to get to know this woman a little better and he had to admit that he did like what he'd glimpsed today.

Sam Monroe wasn't nearly as stuck-up or empty-headed as he'd initially thought. As a matter of fact, in all fairness, he had to admit that she wasn't either one of these things. At the end of the day, she was a pretty decent sort of person.

"You're welcome," he mumbled. Reaching his truck, he got in on his side, waiting for her to follow suit on the passenger side. "If we hurry," he told her, "we can make dinner."

"You mean we might be late?" She hadn't realized they were cutting it this close. Why hadn't he said anything? At the very least, they could have skipped Murphy's. She could have always met the owners at some other time.

"We might be," he allowed, turning on the ignition. "You never know what can happen."

Had he pulled her leg for some reason she couldn't fathom at the moment?

"What time is dinner again?" she asked.

He glanced at his watch. "In half an hour," he told her mildly.

Her eyes widened. "Why didn't you *say* something?" Sam demanded in frustration. There was nothing she hated more than being late unless it was keeping someone waiting, which was the opposite side of the being late coin.

"I just figured you wouldn't want me to rush you, seeing as how we're on so much better footing now than we were this morning," he told her loftily. Mike stepped on the accelerator and the speedometer began to climb correspondingly.

Sam had no idea if he was being serious, or if they'd slid back to square one and he was just mocking her again and being sarcastic. She found that with Mike, it was hard to tell.

Sam crossed her fingers and hoped for the best— on all fronts.

MIGUEL WAS OUT on the porch, pacing, his eyes never leaving the darkened road, when the truck finally came into view as it drove toward the house.

Finally.

Nothing had befallen them, Miguel thought with no small relief.

The older man's face lit up the moment he saw them. He was hurrying down the three steps, wanting to meet them, as Mike parked his vehicle and turned off the ignition.

"I was beginning to worry that something had happened," Miguel called out, raising his voice to be heard above the engine. When Mike turned it off, he lowered his voice accordingly. "You have been gone a long time," Miguel observed. "And you forgot to take your cell phone again," he told his son, his eyes narrowing momentarily in exasperation.

"I didn't forget," Mike corrected his father. "I just

didn't take it." Leaving it behind had been a matter of choice as far as he was concerned.

"My son does not like modern conveniences," Miguel explained to his houseguest haplessly.

"It's not a convenience," Mike countered. "It's a damn *inconvenience* to be hounded every time I turn a corner, what with the ringing and the buzzing and all those other noises the damn thing makes."

"That's the music," Ray informed him, coming to the doorway to greet Sam. He smiled at her as he told his brother, "And that's also the text buzzer just letting you know that someone sent you a text message."

Mike had no patience with all these new ways to communicate. In his estimation, there was nothing wrong with the old way and he was a firm believer in the "If it's not broke, don't fix it" adage.

"Someone wants to send me a message," he growled, "they can call me like everyone else."

"What good would that do if you keep leaving your cell phone lying around every chance you get?" Ray asked him.

"You've got a point," Mike agreed. "I'm going to have to think about that a bit to come up with an answer," he deadpanned. "In the meantime, let's eat before we starve our houseguest here," he concluded, jerking a thumb in Sam's direction.

She noticed she was "their" houseguest when it meant that Mike would get something out of the argument.

That just might be a point worth remembering, Sam thought.

Chapter Eight

The dinner was excellent. His housekeeper had out-done herself, but Miguel's mind was not on what was on his plate, but on the young woman seated to his left at his table.

He found her to be lively, engaging and amusing. In short, he liked her. Liked her a great deal. She was enthusiastic about the project that lay ahead of her, had intelligent questions about the town she had toured today and he sensed she was being genuine about wanting to find a way to help the Native Americans who either chose to remain on the reservation or, due to circumstances they were not able to control or change, were forced to remain there even if they would have preferred to leave and forge their own path.

Though he hadn't actually experienced any uneasiness about it previously, he now felt that his decision to entrust his great-great-great-grandmother's story to this small slip of a thing had been a good one.

Finished with dinner, Miguel moved his plate back. "So, if you have no objections," he said, continuing to address Sam, "I would like you to begin reading the diaries tomorrow morning. I want your honest opinion about the wisdom of turning the journals into a book for my grandchildren to read someday."

"Absolutely," Sam quickly agreed with enthusiasm. With the ease of someone accustomed to caring for herself and effortlessly handling all the details that went into running a household, Sam began to clear away and stack up the dishes as she went on talking with her new employer. "But if it is all the same to you, I'd rather get started tonight, not tomorrow morning," she told him, taking Mike's dish and placing it on top of her own. Leaving both sets of cutlery on top, she reached for Miguel's.

"Tonight?" Miguel echoed. Her request caught him off guard. "I would think that you would want to rest, get a good night's sleep first, before facing all that tedious work—some of the writing is very faint and difficult to make out," he warned.

She reached for Ray's plate as well as his knife and fork, slipping the plate beneath the other plates while depositing the cutlery with the rest that she was accumulating on top.

"I'm much too excited about getting to read her journals to sleep, Miguel," she confessed to him. "So if you have no objections, I'd appreciate you letting me see them tonight so I can at least glance through what I'll be facing tomorrow."

She really *was* the right choice, Miguel thought happily. "If that is what you wish," he told her, inclining his head. Then, unable to ignore her piling up the dishes any longer, he finally asked, "What *are* you doing?"

She was so involved in the project they were talking about, for a moment Sam didn't know what Miguel's question referred to. She blinked, about to ask him what he meant, then realized he was watching her hands. Belatedly, she realized he had to be asking her about the dishes she was gathering.

"Clearing the table," she answered simply.

"Why?" Miguel asked, somewhat mystified. This was what Alma did on occasion when she came for lunch or dinner. But guests did not do chores.

Sam was the face of innocence as she answered, "Because we're through eating and the dishes were just sitting there."

Rather than Miguel, it was Mike who rose and put his hand on her wrist to stop her from reaching for any more dishes. As she looked at him quizzically, he took the pile of plates with its cutlery out of her hands and placed the entire collection on the table.

"I think what Dad's trying to say is that you're his houseguest, not the new maid he hired," Mike informed her sternly.

"I don't mind doing my share," Sam said cheerfully, deliberately addressing her words to Miguel and not the man standing in her way.

"Your 'share,'" Mike told her pointedly, moving the plates out of her reach in case she had intentions of picking them up again, "will be going over the diaries, not clearing the table or putting the dishes into the dishwasher."

The last part caught her attention and she looked at Mike. "I wasn't going to put the dishes into the dishwasher," she told him.

"Oh?" He didn't believe her, but he was curious to hear what she was going to say.

"No, I was going to wash them myself," she said.

Before Mike could say something derogatory, she turned her attention to Miguel and said, "Washing dishes helps me clear my head."

Her explanation was also an appeal to the older man for understanding. There were reasons behind her doing what she did and she wanted to be free to follow her instincts, no matter how trivial they might sound to someone else.

Miguel spread his hands in a gesture that was meant to remove him from the center of the confrontation. "If you find that it really helps you, then how can I tell you not to do it?" Miguel asked with an indulgent smile.

Sam's eyes smiled her thanks as a warm wave of kinship washed over her. She reached for the plates again, picking them up so that she could finally take them into the kitchen. She paused just for a moment before Miguel's chair.

"If I could have picked a father," she told the patriarch, "he would have been just like you."

"I am flattered," Miguel said. Then her words replayed themselves in his head. They took on more import. "Wait, you never knew your father?" he asked.

Sam shook her head. "No, I was never that lucky," she replied, directing her words toward Mike before she disappeared into the kitchen.

Miguel looked after her thoughtfully before he turned his attention back to his sons. "Did you hear what Samantha said? Consider yourselves lucky," he said to his sons, pretending to be serious.

"Well, I do," Ray readily declared, looking off in the direction Sam had gone in. "Lucky to be living in a house where that hot little number is going to be staying—how long is she supposed to be here again?" he asked, looking from his father to Mike, waiting for an answer and obviously hoping that the woman's stay would be a lengthy one.

"Too long," was Mike's response while Miguel told his youngest, "About six weeks was what she had told me." And then Miguel frowned at Ray. While he loved all his children equally for different reasons, his youngest was a test to his patience. There were times when it seemed as if Ramon went through a woman a week. At this point, Forever had run out of potential marital partners—he'd been with every woman under ninety except for Miss Joan.

"Ramon," Miguel warned his son, "you are to be a gentleman."

"Nothing less crossed my mind, Dad," Ray told his father with a grin, elaborately crossing his heart for his father's benefit. "You don't have dibs on her or anything, right?" he asked Mike.

In response, Mike uttered something under his breath akin to a growl.

Ray interpreted the disgruntled sound to mean what he wanted it to. "Okay, then, I'll take that as a no." His grin broadened. It was the same grin that so many women found to be fatally charming. "Which means that she's fair game—"

"You listen to me and you listen good," Mike said to his brother in a low, steely voice that left no room for any doubt. "She's not any kind of a 'game,' she's a person. A person Dad hired to do a specific job. You're not going to hang around her, you're not going to annoy her and you're not going to get in her way in any manner, shape or form. You're going to let her do her job and then she's going to take her money, her single suitcase and her laptop and she's going to go—is that clear?"

"What are you getting so bent out of shape about?" Ray asked.

"Because there's got to be at least one woman left in the state that you haven't—and *won't*—put your mark on. Think of it as a challenge," he ordered his brother. His implication was clear. Either Ray left Sam alone, or he would *make* Ray leave her alone. "Now is that clear?" he repeated.

"Clear," Ray mumbled, obviously not overjoyed to be giving this answer.

"Good."

With that, Mike walked out of the house.

There was nothing but stunned silence in Mike's wake lingering in the dining room for at least a couple of minutes.

And then Miguel banished the silence by venturing a guess. "I think that your brother is interested in our houseguest."

Ray laughed, but rather than deny his father's assumption, he heartily reinforced it.

"Oh, yeah. Big-time," he agreed, bobbing his head up and down. "Don't think I've ever seen big brother quite this edgy before, either," Ray went on to observe.

"That is because Miguel never liked being restricted, and caring about someone restricts a person, it puts up boundaries."

"This," Ray predicted just before he left the room himself, "should be very interesting."

WHICH WAS THE exact thought that Sam had a little while later, after she had finished the dishes over

Rosa's very vocal protests. As she put the last dish away, Miguel called her into the living room. When she came in, he showed her the dust-encrusted box filled with the diaries and journals he had discovered during his quest to organize and clean up the attic.

If he still had the slightest bit of doubt lingering about hiring someone so young to tackle something of such importance to him, she hoped that she had obliterated it with her reverence for the box and its contents.

"It's like touching history," she told him in a hushed voice.

Miguel nodded, no doubt pleased to hear her describe it that way.

"You did say that you wanted to get started tonight," he reminded her. His tone almost sounded like an apology for showing her the journals.

"Oh, yes, of course. Absolutely," she said with feeling.

Feeling almost beside herself with anticipation, Sam didn't know where to begin. She felt she had to do this just right. Her other projects had been very different in comparison. Doing those she would take what were at times disjointed scenes and endless pages of incoherent ramblings and turn them into a coherent, interesting whole that in turn drew its share of devoted readers.

But in each case, she was dealing with contemporary biographies, written about and supposedly by famous or semifamous people of the present day. None of them represented a sense of history, there was no feeling of reaching across the bridge of time to touch another world that had long since faded away.

This project, however, was different.

This project was *important*.

Realizing that her host probably thought she'd been struck dumb, Sam looked up at him, flashed a smile and asked, "Where can I work? I'm going to need some room to take the books out and go through them, perhaps arrange them chronologically without crowding them in case the bindings are flimsy—which they probably are," she suddenly realized.

They were over a hundred and fifty years old; how could they be anything but fragile and flimsy?

"You can work in the study," Miguel immediately offered. The study had a good, sturdy desk, its walls were lined with shelves overflowing with books and the morning light was excellent in that room. It was the perfect place to work.

Overhearing, Mike was quick to protest the study being lost to him. "Dad, that's where I've got the accounting books for the ranch."

His objection implied more than that to her. It meant that he did whatever paperwork he had to for the ranch in this room.

She didn't want to throw Mike out of what was clearly his office. "Maybe I can just bring the journals and diaries up to my room."

She tried to remember if there was a desk in that room. There had to be, right? And if there wasn't, Sam decided in the next minute, she could certainly improvise. Even when she was a little girl, she'd never been one to be hemmed in by just one idea, just one approach to a problem. Flexibility had always been the key in everything she did.

"No need," Miguel told her. He looked at his oldest. "Surely you can work out a schedule where you will not be in each other's way."

"Of course," she agreed immediately. "You just tell me when you need the space and I'll be sure to make myself scarce."

Mike sincerely doubted that she could accomplish something like that. She hadn't even been there a day and he could already tell if she'd been in the room by the scent of her perfume or cologne or whatever it was that smelled like a combination of honeysuckle and her.

"See?" his father asked in response to Sam's offer to share office time. "You cannot ask for anything better than that."

Yeah, he could, Mike thought.

He could ask for this woman not to be around at all. He could ask for his world not to be disturbed, to continue just the way it had been going, letting him run the ranch for the most part while his brothers and sister did whatever it was that they did—which these days usually meant getting married and having babies. He had no interest in either.

He neither wanted to have his own happiness depend on the happiness of someone else—he'd seen enough of his brothers' entanglements to know that was the way it went—nor did he yearn to have a tiny human being suddenly roaming the earth composed of his genes and someone else's. He was perfectly content keeping to himself and doing what he was good at—which in this case meant running the family ranch.

"Yeah, whatever," he murmured in response to Sam's suggestion.

Mike started to leave the room, only to have his father foil his getaway by saying, "Miguel here will take these books into the study for you."

He was offering Sam a warm body to do her bidding, Mike thought, disgruntled.

"That's all right," Sam was quick to refuse the offer. "I can do it. I'm stronger than I look," she added when she saw the older man open his mouth to protest her doing any such thing.

"I am sure that you are," Miguel replied diplomatically. "But indulge an old man—I would prefer to have my son take these books into the study for you than to watch you bend beneath their burden." He turned toward his son. "Miguel?"

Mike made no reply. Instead of talking, he picked up the box in one sweeping motion.

It was a damn sight heavier than it looked, but he was determined not to make a sound.

Only when he had the box properly balanced did Mike look expectantly at his father. "Any particular place in the study?"

Instead of answering his son, Miguel looked toward Sam. "Perhaps you should accompany him into the study," he suggested. "Then you can have Miguel put the books where you can best get to them and they will not be in your way—or his," he added, glancing at Mike, "when you are working on something else."

Exactly what else did he expect her to be working on, Sam wondered, then decided that he was probably referring to Mike's work, not hers.

The old man was up to something, Mike thought. And it didn't take a brilliant mind to guess what.

Too bad the old man was going to be disappointed

because no way was he going to be matched up with anyone, even a woman as attractive and as self-sufficient as this one was. The fact that she didn't ask to be indulged or placated, didn't play the part of the helpless little woman, were all points in her favor, as was the fact that she was probably the prettiest woman he'd ever seen up close and personal.

But he wasn't in the market for a better half or any half at all.

He was in the market for peace and quiet, something, he had a hunch, he wasn't going to be able to get much of for the next six weeks—if not longer because as far as he knew, she could very well draw the whole process out.

He told himself to focus on the light at the end of the tunnel, even if that tunnel seemed to be damn long right now.

"You coming?" he asked in an exasperated voice. Not waiting for an answer, Mike walked out of the living room and headed toward the study.

The sound of clicking heels on tile told him she was right behind him.

He allowed himself a slight, momentary smile. Getting her to act the way he wanted her to wasn't all that difficult, he thought. All he needed was the right incentive, the right bait and this potential one-hundred-and-ten-pound problem would be no problem at all.

Or at least he could hope.

Chapter Nine

Sam realized that she kept losing track of time. Not just for a few hours or once in a while, but what amounted to every day for the past three weeks. She was that immersed in her work.

The whole thing was akin to stumbling across one of those wonderful books that pulled you in the moment you first opened it, propelling you into a world that was far removed from your own and just too exciting to leave. That was how she began to work every morning. Once started, she really hated to put whatever journal she was reading down and the temptation to just "turn another page," "read another passage," or "come down to the end of the next paragraph" was just too seductive for her to voluntarily stop.

Since she'd begun wading through the various diaries, journals and the collection of independent notations that were made years later—if the difference in handwriting and quality of the paper were any indication—Sam had found that she had a hard time remembering to stop reading in order to get something to eat.

Time ceased to have any significance for her because she wasn't running according to current schedules or timepieces. She was back approximately one hundred and forty-five years in the past, feeling the emotions of a girl more than ten years her junior. Each fear Marguerite experienced became *her* fear, each moment of heart-racing anticipation became hers, as well.

When she read these journals, it felt as if she *were* Marguerite.

It had been like this for three weeks. She only stopped when someone knocked on the door of the study, more likely than not startling her, to announce that it was time for lunch or dinner. Some of the time, the messenger who pulled her back into the twenty-first century was Miguel or Rosa. But of late, she'd noticed that Miguel—she was certain he had to be the one behind this change as to who was coming to fetch her—had Mike call her back to the present-day world.

This time around, it took more than a passing knock, or even a loud one to rouse her. It took persistent knocking, not because she was so utterly wrapped up in what she was reading but because she'd fallen asleep over the journal she'd been reading and studying so closely the past few hours.

Three weeks of little to no sleep had finally caught up to her and the last thing she remembered was that her eyelids had suddenly each weighed approximately one ton apiece.

Startled, she sat up, trying to focus her foggy brain as quickly as possible. When she did, she realized that Mike was no longer merely knocking on the door. He had opened it and walked in.

"Found a new way to absorb what's written in those books?" he asked her, amused.

Still half-asleep, Sam stared at him, trying desperately to orient her brain to her surroundings. A moment earlier, she'd been running through the forest, trying to elude a stray band of renegades who had just killed her entire family.

Somehow, her own family, which technically consisted of her mother and the man her mother had married, the man who had whisked her mother off to another state before the ink was dry on the marriage license, had blended with Marguerite's family. It was *those* people she had lost, those people she'd been mourning as she ran breathlessly through the woods, trying to save herself from being kidnapped—or worse.

In her dream, she'd lost sight of where Marguerite ended and she began. For a moment, before her surroundings started coming into focus, she'd been embedded in a world that had been gone for close to a hundred and fifty years now.

Returning to the present, to the study in a ranch house in Forever, Texas, wasn't as easy as it might have seemed at first.

Mike's words made no sense to her, even when she replayed them in her head. Clearing her throat, which felt as if it was clogged with dust mites, she asked, "What?"

"Your face," he pointed out with more amusement than she'd seen him display since she'd arrived in Forever, "it was plastered against the journal. I thought that maybe you'd found a new way to absorb the story faster."

His words finally penetrated.

"Oh, my God."

Sam's eyes widened in stunned horror as she realized what she'd done. Her head was on the desk, which meant that she'd rested her cheek against the pages of the journal she'd been reading when she'd dropped off to sleep.

Her hand flew to her face. There were natural oils on the skin that could have easily come off onto the pages that were opened and stained them, causing the writing, which was faint in some places to begin with, to blur.

Her heart sank at the prospect that she could have damaged the journal.

"What's the matter?" Mike asked, looking around the room, wondering what she could have just seen to set her off like this. As far as he could see, nothing appeared to be out of place.

"I could have ruined some pages," she cried, picking up the journal and holding the pages she'd just been napping on up to the light.

Mike looked at her, apparently not seeing why she should be panicking about the matter.

"What's a few pages when there're obviously so many?" he asked, gesturing toward the other journals that were piled up on the other end of the desk.

Sam shook her head. How could he be so cavalier? These pages represented *history*. Damn it, she didn't even remember being sleepy and she certainly didn't remember laying down her head on the journal.

"But these pages could have been crucial to Marguerite's story," she argued, really angry with herself.

"Highly unlikely," he speculated. When she looked at him incredulously, he merely pointed to the other journals again. "Two pages out of all those. Just think about the odds."

It was hard to think of anything at all when her stomach was all tied up in a nervous, horrified knot the way it was right now. But she forced herself to examine the pages in question closely and that in turn allowed the knot in her stomach to loosen considerably. None of the words appeared to be any more blurred than they had been initially.

Sam breathed a long sigh of relief. "I didn't hurt it."

Something struck him as funny about that and Mike laughed shortly. "Didn't hurt it?" he echoed, then said to the contrary, "You probably did it some good. That's probably the closest those pages've come to seeing some sort of life in centuries."

"The journal is only a century and a half old," Sam pointed out. Her eyes skimmed over the two pages in question again—just to be sure they were all right and that fear hadn't blinded her.

It hadn't. She could still make out every word of the small, extremely precise handwriting. For once she was grateful that her skin was in need of moisturizing.

He shrugged. "Whatever," he muttered dismissively. "Okay, now that the emergency has been canceled, why don't you come to dinner?" he suggested. "Dad's getting concerned about you and he sure as hell isn't paying you enough to have you sequestering yourself in his study with his dead relative for hours on end every day without any kind of a break."

That almost made her sound like a prisoner, she thought. "That's not exactly the way I see it," Sam pointed out.

"Then take another look," Mike told her, his voice emotionless but firm. Since she still appeared to need further encouragement, he reminded her, "The journals aren't going anywhere and the old man enjoys the company of a pretty girl. Makes him feel that he's not as old as his birth certificate tells him he is."

"Woman," Sam said.

Back at the door, his hand on the doorknob, Mike stopped to look at her, confused. "Excuse me?"

"Woman," Sam repeated. "You said 'girl.' I'm a woman."

He watched her for a long moment, his eyes sweeping over the length of her slowly. She was wearing a pair of slim jeans that accentuated more than hid. The button-down work shirt she had on made her look more like an impish kid than the woman she claimed to be.

But there was *no* mistaking the very tempting swell that was causing the top closed button on her shirt to strain as it struggled to remain in place.

"Yeah, maybe you are one at that," he said appreciatively.

His tone made her blush and Sam damned herself for it. She needed a few minutes alone so she could pull herself together. "Why don't you tell your father I'll be there in a few minutes?"

Mike sighed impatiently and strode back into the study, crossing to the desk and lining himself up behind her chair.

"I've got a better idea," he told her, angling the chair so that it was parallel to the doorway. "Why don't I just deliver you to the old man myself?"

It wasn't so much a question as a statement of intent. The next moment, Sam found herself being wheeled toward the doorway and the hallway that was just beyond.

"Wait," she pleaded. "Leave the chair," Sam told him as she jumped off it, giving him no excuse to move the chair any farther from where it had initially been placed.

But the next moment, to her embarrassment, Sam realized she hadn't fully cleared the chair and her left heel got caught against the chair's back wheels. As a result, she stumbled as she tried to stand and lost her balance.

She would have fallen, most likely flat on her ego as well as her face, had Mike not acted on instinct and made an automatic grab for her.

Hands on her shoulders, he pulled Sam in the opposite direction, negating her fall.

Sort of.

One moment she'd been attempting to clear a chair, the next she was inches from Mike, looking up into his face. Into his eyes specifically—and seeing all sorts of things she hadn't thought could exist within the man.

Deep things, timeless things.

Things that seemed to, just for a moment, rivet her in place and steal her breath away even *before* he did what he did next.

Why he did it would remain a mystery to Mike for a very long time to come. As a rule, he wasn't given to acting on impulse. He always took the high road, accepting the fact that he was above such impulses, such urges, and as far as he knew, he was.

Except this one time.

One moment, he was just doing what came instinctively, in this case breaking her fall. The next, he was doing something that came naturally to others.

He was kissing her.

He wasn't even aware of the need for this sensual contact rising up within him. As far as Mike could assess, he was catching her but then she was catching him, at least figuratively.

There was no other way to explain it. At that particular moment in time, he needed to be doing *exactly* what he was doing. Pressing his lips against hers, drawing in her essence and making it one with his.

Samantha Monroe tasted of laughter and sweetness and impossible things he couldn't begin to understand. And the longer his lips were against hers, the longer he *wanted* them to be against hers.

The simple, spontaneous action brought with it a huge surge the likes of which he couldn't remember *ever* experiencing before. And, most likely, since he had no intentions of acting impulsively like this for a second time, he never would again.

But while he was here, wrapped up in this kiss, he told himself he might as well drink it in, absorbing it the way he had just teased her about absorbing the page her face had been pressed against when she'd fallen asleep on it.

Except that in his case, he *wanted* to absorb her, to taste and feel her essence, her soul with his.

IF SHE DIDN'T know any better, Sam would have sworn that she was still dreaming. Except that now, she wasn't being pursued by a marauding band of renegades bent on her destruction but had fallen headlong into a place she had only read about because it resembled no kiss she'd experienced before.

Her first instinct was to pull away, but it was

quickly superseded by a desire to remain just where she was, lost in the moment.

The boys and men who had kissed her in her lifetime—especially Daniel—had caused her heart to flutter mainly *before* the act. Actually, it was the anticipation of the kiss that had always caused her heart and pulse to react the way it did, to speed up.

But once flesh touched flesh and the thought became a reality, it was almost always anchored by disappointment. She'd found that the actual deed *never* lived up to the dream, even when love was involved—because she had loved her late husband. Loved him for the good man he was, not for the way he had made her blood surge in her veins—because, she admitted in the deepest chamber of her heart, he hadn't.

She'd accepted that, learned to live with it and taught herself to tone down her expectations. That allowed her to be content with what she had. And when cruel circumstances had dictated that she no longer had it, Sam hadn't gone looking for a replacement because there was no crying physical need to reclaim paradise since she'd never been to paradise in the first place.

Not until now.

Now she'd glimpsed it, and been made aware of its existence. Her suddenly rediscovered anticipation whispered in her ear that there was now something very real to dream about.

WHAT THE HELL had gotten into him? a voice inside Mike's head demanded incredulously as well as angrily.

Had he lost his mind?

He'd come to fetch Sam for dinner, not jump on her like some polecat trying to scale a tree to get a better view of his surroundings. Where had this sudden urge, this need to taste her lips, her very soul, come from? He had more control over himself than that, Mike silently insisted.

So, just as abruptly as he'd begun kissing her, he stopped, pulling his head back and stepping away from her. The very last thing he did was drop his hands from her shoulders, as if somehow sensing on some level that she'd sink unsteadily to her knees if his hands were no longer there to hold her up.

Sorry.

"Sorry," he said louder, unsure if he'd already said the word out loud or if he'd only thought it and it hadn't made it past his lips.

"Nothing to apologize for," she told him, her voice scarcely above a shaky whisper. "Especially not two times."

Okay, he thought, he *had* said it twice. Just showed him how shaken up his brain really was at the moment. Guilt scraped across his conscience like a jagged, rusty nail. "I'd hate to think that I—"

Sam squared her shoulders, no longer dazed, no longer mesmerized. And she didn't want to hear what he had to say.

"You apologize again and I won't be held responsible for my reaction," she informed him tersely.

She didn't want to hear him denounce what had to be the singular most spectacular kiss she'd ever experienced, bar none. Not to mention that for the first time since Danny's death, she'd actually felt alive on more than the putting-one-foot-in-front-of-the-other level that had, thus far, been seeing her through this enormously dark period of her life.

As a matter of fact, despite his clumsy attempts at both an apology and obvious denial, her heart was still racing.

Sam savored the sensation for a moment longer, fully aware that it was even now beginning to fade, drawing away from her grasp.

Clearing her throat as she raised her eyes to his, she made a valiant stab at normalcy.

"You said something about dinner," she reminded him. "What about it?" Because, for the life of her, other than knowing he'd said the word, she couldn't remember anything beyond that.

Mike did his best to strip away the last of the effects of what had just happened here between them. "It's waiting."

Now it came back to her. He'd been trying to literally roll her out of the room when she'd jumped out of the chair and somehow into his arms.

"Oh, right. Well, let's not keep it waiting any longer," she murmured, walking by him to the door.

Mike turned on his heel and followed her and the tantalizing scent that seemed to cling to her, wondering if he was coming down with something and should have himself checked out. More than anything, he needed an answer, an excuse to cling to that he could live with.

And the sooner, the better.

Chapter Ten

The moment Sam walked into the dining room Miguel was on his feet and headed straight for her.

"Ah, there you are. I was beginning to think you had gotten lost," the patriarch said to her, warmly taking her hand between his as he uttered the greeting. Then, releasing it, he took her elbow and gently guided her to the table, which was set for four. "You cannot neglect yourself this way time and again," Miguel chided kindly. "You must eat, otherwise how can you keep up your strength to do all this work?"

Sam laughed as she took her chair, then expressed a twinge of surprise when Mike pulled it out for her. When she was seated, he pushed the chair in for her, as well. This wave of politeness was new. Obviously this was due to his father's prompting, she thought.

Their eyes met for a brief instant as Mike went to take his own seat.

What she saw in his eyes made her change her mind. Maybe Mike's father hadn't had anything to do with Mike's change in behavior. Maybe that kiss, coming out of nowhere, was responsible for the difference.

Did this mean that he intended to repeat that encounter?

God, she hoped so.

Belatedly, Sam realized that she hadn't responded to what her host had just said to her. "It's not as if I'm doing some kind of heavy physical labor, Miguel," she reminded him tactfully. "It's just reading."

They both knew it wasn't "just" anything. He looked at her knowingly. "Using the mind for all those hours can be very tiring."

"Yeah, just look at Mike. He almost never tires himself out thinking about anything," Ray offered, laughing at his own joke.

"Mike keeps the books, doesn't he?" Sam asked casually.

Out of the corner of her eye, she saw the surprised expression on Mike's face. That was when she realized that she had to sound as if she was coming to his defense. What had prompted her to do that? It wasn't as if the man couldn't defend himself. But then, maybe he wasn't inclined to offer any justification that wasn't already duly recognized and noted.

"Well, it sounds like Samantha put you in your place, Ramon," Miguel observed, a deep, appreciative chuckle accompanying his words.

In response, Ray shrugged somewhat self-consciously, doing his best not to appear that way.

"Doesn't take much to work on the books," he protested, then complained, "I don't do it because you won't let me."

"And there's a good reason for that," Mike deadpanned, joining in. "You don't let someone who thinks one plus one equals eleven work on the accounts, unless you think that risking bankruptcy is a good idea."

Ray bristled. "Don't listen to him," he told Sam. "He doesn't know what he's talking about."

She realized that Ray was embarrassed and she was quick to try to remedy the situation. Smiling at him, Sam said, "That's all right, not everyone is good with numbers. I'm sure you're not as bad as he thinks— and possibly not as good as you think," she added.

"Ah, she has you there, son," Miguel told his youngest with a laugh, delighted with Sam's breezy assessment.

Taking up his carving knife and fork, Miguel paused to slice an extra thick portion of the prime rib he'd had Rosa prepare. Carefully placing the piece on Sam's plate, he went on to cut several slices, one each for his sons and himself.

Reseating himself, Miguel focused his attention on his houseguest again. "So, tell me, Samantha, how is the work on the journals going?"

"Very well," she answered with genuine enthusiasm. "I'm even further along reading the diaries than I thought I would be." At this rate, she could very well be finished under her projected six-week schedule.

"Good," Miguel proclaimed, extremely pleased. "That means you will not object when I ask you to take a little break."

"I thought that was what I was doing," she said, indicating the meal she was having.

"I think what Dad means is an actual break, not just dinner," Mike interjected, although he kept his eyes on his plate.

An actual break. I thought that was what happened back in the study, Sam couldn't help thinking.

Because what happened back there was certainly not business as usual.

A shiver danced down her back even as she thought of the kiss. She forced herself to focus on the conversation and not on her reaction to the unexpected, pulse-stirring event.

"Miguel is right," the older man agreed. "I mean an *actual* break. People like Miss Joan," he cited the diner owner specifically because Miss Joan asked the most questions, "are asking me if I am keeping you trapped in the study, working."

"I'm not trapped," Sam protested. "The door's not locked. Besides, I'm enjoying reading these diaries immensely. Your great-great-great-grandmother was a very brave young woman," she told Miguel. "That she found a way to write down some of these details, even while they kept her as pretty much a slave, is just absolutely amazing to me."

"Strong women *are* amazing," Miguel agreed. "But as I am sure you know, work, while important, is not everything. There are other things, such as friends, family," he enumerated, his eyes watching her carefully. "Speaking of family," he segued just a little too innocently. "Where is yours?"

Seeing Sam's discomfort at the question, although she was quick to cover it up, Mike interceded for her and told his father, "She doesn't have any family around here. She doesn't have any brothers or sisters and when her mother remarried, she and her new husband moved away to another state. She and Sam lost contact."

A number of emotions crossed the older man's face,

not the least of which was sympathy. "Is this true, Samantha?" he asked.

"Yes." She really hadn't thought that Mike remembered. She'd told him about her lack of family on the first day. She was sure it had gone in one ear and out the other. To find out it didn't rather intrigued her. There was a great deal more to this man than she thought. He actually *did* listen. On occasion.

"Then am I correct to think that you have no plans for the holiday?" Miguel asked her.

"Holiday?" she echoed. The question threw her. "Do you mean Christmas?"

Why was he asking about that? With any luck, she would be finished and gone before Christmas arrived.

As a rule, Sam didn't look forward to the Christmas holiday. It always reminded her how alone she was. Oh, she knew she could always ignore the holiday—which was difficult in light of the endless commercials and the decorated department stores. Or she could thrust herself into someone's party—her publisher always threw one—and hope the noise would blot out her thoughts. But she really didn't want to intrude on anyone she knew, especially since she really wasn't close enough to the people she did know to inject herself into their celebrations.

Christmas with its festivities, frantic shopping and extra dose of cheer was always especially hard on her. It made her long for what she didn't have. A family.

Rousing herself, she realized that Miguel was shaking his head.

"Actually," he told her, "I am talking about Thanksgiving Day. Am I correct to think that you have no plans?"

"I have no plans," Sam echoed, then regretted it. The last thing she wanted was to have this man feel as if he had to invite her to his family's gathering. "But don't worry, I won't interfere with yours."

"Excuse me?" he said, exchanging looks with his sons. The word she had used confused him.

Before she could repeat her answer, Mike took over the conversation. "I think my father is trying to tell you that he'd like you to come and have Thanksgiving dinner with us."

"I am very capable of saying that for myself, Miguel," Miguel informed his oldest son, then turned to look at Sam, "But yes, I was trying to—how do you say—feel you up for the holidays?"

"Out, Dad, you were trying to feel her *out* about the holidays," Mike quickly corrected.

Ray would have beaten him to it, but his youngest brother was laughing so hard at the moment he couldn't talk.

Miguel threw up his hands. "Up, out, what is the difference?"

"There's a difference, Dad," Mike assured him. "Trust me."

Miguel glanced at his young guest and said with confidence, "She knows what I mean. So, will you do me—will you do *us*," he corrected, gesturing around the table at his two sons as well as himself, "the honor of joining us for Thanksgiving dinner—if you have no plans," he qualified again.

For a moment, Sam seriously thought of coming up with an excuse, saying she'd forgotten that she had promised to meet with some friends over Thanksgiving, but the truth of it was, the prospect of taking that special meal with this family proved to be more than a little tempting. *Especially* in light of the way she felt about being alone for Thanksgiving.

She could remember the way she felt one year at Thanksgiving when she and her mother were walking past a diner. Looking in, she saw a man sitting alone on a stool at the counter, slowly eating his turkey dinner. She could almost taste it sticking to the roof of his mouth.

She'd felt incredibly sorry for that man in the diner and now, since Danny had died and her mother hadn't expressed any desire to reconnect with her, she realized that she *was* that man in the diner.

Except that now she had an option. She didn't have to be that lonely man at the counter if she didn't want to be.

"I'd love to join you—if you're sure that I wouldn't be putting you out," she qualified.

Miguel shook his head, puzzled as to where she would get that idea. "I would not be inviting you if I felt you would be putting me 'out,' as you say."

Sam looked at him. Her eyes held Miguel's and she smiled. "Yes, you would," she contradicted. "Because you're a very kind man."

Ray laughed. "He's not all *that* kind," the young man assured her. "As a matter of fact, there're times he can be downright hard-nosed about things."

Mike slanted a glance in his brother's direction. "And yet, you still continue being the disappointment you are," Mike deadpanned in a low voice.

Miguel looked up sharply. "Miguel," the older man's voice had a warning note in it. A note that said he would not put up with being crossed.

Mike spread his hands wide and was the picture of innocence. "I'm just telling it the way it is, Dad, nothing more."

Miguel turned toward her, a weary look on his face. "If you wish to turn me down," Miguel said to her, "because my sons have no manners, I will understand. My heart will be heavy," he qualified with a sigh, "but I will understand."

Sam laughed, truly delighted to be part of this warm, friendly group of people, however briefly. Cocking her head, she looked at her host's expression. "There is no *way* I could say no to that face," she told Miguel in all honesty.

The patriarch watched her with the most hopeful pair of eyes she had ever seen. The only eyes that had come remotely close to that look had belonged to a puppy she'd had as a little girl—before he'd run off after she and her mother had moved in the dead of night because they were behind in their rent.

"He's counting on that, you know," Mike told her, then went on to attest, "I've seen him practicing that face in the mirror."

Miguel's eyes narrowed as he glared at his namesake. "I am beginning to think that Samantha is not the only one who is spending too much time by themselves. At least she is reading your honored ancestor's words. You have no one to communicate with except for the horses and the fence posts," Miguel lamented, shaking his head sorrowfully at his oldest son.

"You've got that right," Ray declared heartily, pleased to have the focus off him. "Mike's just a couple of steps removed from being a crazy old hermit," he confided to Sam.

Miguel seemed pleased that his youngest agreed with him. "Good, you think so, too," he said to Ray. "Which is why I believe you should trade positions with Miguel for a few weeks," the older man told Ray.

Ray appeared as if he was about to choke on his dinner. "What?"

"You actually want us to switch jobs?" Mike asked his father.

"Yes," Miguel said with feeling, obviously glad he was being understood. He pointed to Ray. "You will take Miguel's place, ride the range, watch over the herd and check for breaks in the fences," he enumerated, "while Miguel will be here, doing whatever it is you do," Miguel said to Ray with a vague wave of his hand.

"I get supplies for the ranch," Ray protested indignantly.

"Yes, and spend all your time doing it," Miguel reminded him.

To which Ray responded with a somewhat defensive, if careless shrug. "It's a big ranch. We need a lot of supplies. That takes time to bring back from town. I don't want to overload the truck. It's old and it might break down."

Sam leaned back, smiling as she listened to the interaction between the three men. She had to confess that she was a little surprised that Mike talked as much as he did—and that he had taken as much note of her as he had.

But then, after what had transpired in the study a little while ago, nothing else should surprise her when it came to the tall, handsome rancher.

Sam caught herself looking at Mike far more than

she looked at the other two men even though she found all three amusing, interesting and highly likable. But Mike was definitely at the top of the list.

Maybe she *had* been sequestered in that room a little too much. It wasn't often that she connected with people the way she had here—and she gave the credit for that entirely to them rather than to herself.

For as long as she could remember, she had always had a hunger to be something more than the person on the outside, looking in, but because of her circumstances, "outside" was where she was most of the time.

At first it had been because she and her mother had lived a partially nomadic life, staying one jump ahead of the bill collector as her mother continued her search for Mr. Right, the man who would ultimately take her away from all this.

The short period she'd spent with Danny had made her think that those days were gone. She had found her own private "inside" where she could stay, safe and warm and happy. But then Danny was killed in a freak accident and she was alone again. It wasn't long before she found herself reverting back to being the lost person she'd once been.

This, she thought, looking around at the three men at the table, was her fantasy come true. She was *part* of something while she was here. These men let her in—Miguel and Ray had done it immediately, but even Mike had eventually come around. They behaved as if they *expected* her to take part in their lives, not hover on the perimeter, looking in.

That meant the world to her.

Realistically, she knew it couldn't continue. She knew that she was just a guest, not really a part of this family who seemed to thrive on bedeviling each other. Despite the teasing and at times the sharp words, it was obvious that they all loved one another and that each would defend the others with their last ounce of strength and their last breath no matter what the nature of the fight.

She felt lucky to be here, just observing.

ONCE DINNER WAS over and she began to rise, Miguel turned quickly to his namesake and said, "Take her out for a walk, Miguel. I believe she needs to smell the night air, to remember that there is a whole world outside of the study and beyond just this house. She has been neglecting it, as well as herself."

She knew that Miguel meant well, but she couldn't just drop everything and go for a stroll. If she gave in to indulgences like that, she would wind up falling behind schedule. Stopping for dinner had already taken enough of a chunk out of her evening.

"Miguel—" she began to protest.

But Miguel had already made up his mind to turn a deaf ear to whatever it was she had to say if it was to attempt to change his mind.

"I am paying you little enough as it is to do this big job. I am certainly *not* paying you enough to be a slave, Samantha." He winked at her. "Go. Walk outside. Breathe in the night air. Miguel will keep you company. Do this for an old man," he requested, looking at her with eyes that were supplicating all on their own.

Sam had no choice but to agree.

"I will," Sam told him with reluctance, feeling guilty and yet enthused at the same time. Then, standing up on her tiptoes, she whispered in the man's ear, "As long as you tell me who this old man is because I don't see him in this room."

Miguel laughed. Taking Sam gently by the arm, the patriarch brought her over to Mike, then elaborately slipped his arm from hers and brought the two of them together.

"Make sure she doesn't go back to work tonight, Miguel," he told his son. "She needs to appreciate her surroundings here and now. Life," Miguel went on to tell the young woman before him, "moves much too fast. Before we know it, many years have just slipped through our fingers. We need to make the most of it now before it is gone." He gestured toward the sliding glass door that led to the area behind the house. "The night is waiting," he told Sam.

She wanted to beg off, to tell him that she was getting to the good part of the narrative in the diaries, but she just didn't have the heart to disappoint Miguel since he seemed so enthusiastic.

"You're right," she agreed. "It is." And with that she and Mike went out through the rear sliding glass door.

Chapter Eleven

Once they were outside, Mike made her an offer that surprised her.

"You know, if you really want to get back to work, we can hurry around to the front of the house and I can sneak you in before Dad hears anything," Mike told her.

Sam shook her head. "No, maybe your father's right. Maybe I have gotten a little too caught up in the work. Besides, it is getting kind of late. I might accidentally miss something that's important if I continue working on the journals tonight.

"I have to admit that your father did surprise me," she went on to confess, silently adding that it had been a night for surprises all around, starting with Mike and her extremely strong reaction to him.

"He can come on a little strong when he believes something wholeheartedly," Mike told her. "Especially now."

"Why especially now?" she asked.

Being on the outside and yearning for connections, she had always had more than her share of natural curiosity about the people she came in contact with.

But ever since she'd arrived in Forever, that healthy streak had gone into overdrive.

"Dad had a heart attack earlier this year," he told her, "right around the beginning of February. I think it's made him extremely aware of everything, grateful for every small thing that goes right. He's been into his 'smell the roses' phase ever since then."

"A heart attack?" Sam echoed, horrified and genuinely concerned. "There's no hospital around here," she realized. At least, she hadn't seen one the couple of times Mike had shown her around.

"No, there's not," Mike confirmed. "Closest one is in Pine Ridge, about fifty, fifty-two miles away from here," he judged. "And, not only that, but at the time Dad had his heart attack, the town's only doctor had taken his first vacation in several years, so he wasn't even around."

Though she'd just left the man a couple of minutes ago and he seemed the picture of health, the thought of the man having gone through all that pain and understandable fear appalled her. Her ability to empathize and place herself in other people's shoes had her feeling extremely vulnerable and fragile. The very thought of what Miguel and his family had endured upset her.

"What did you do?" she asked Mike, her voice dropping down to a whisper.

"Me, personally, nothing," Mike admitted. He had never felt so helpless in his life—or so worried. He prided himself on being in control of situations and in this one, he clearly was not. He never wanted to be at the mercy of events like that again. "To be honest, I didn't know what to do in that kind of a situation—

although I've taken lessons in CPR since then—we all have," he added. "Dad's in great health now, but it never hurts to be prepared."

The minute the doctor came back with his family, Mike had been quick to fill him in, asking the man to give him a few pointers. Daniel Davenport did better than that. He held an informative class for them, wholeheartedly agreeing that knowing the proper application of CPR was a skill that was well worth learning.

"It happened at dinner and all I can say is that it was damn lucky for Dad that Gabe brought his new girlfriend and her mother to dinner that night because it was Val's mother, some former movie star who Dad had always been sweet on, who wound up saving his life." He laughed softly. "For months, he'd tell anyone who listened—and a lot of people who didn't after a while—that Gloria Halladay saved his life."

Realizing that the name probably meant as little to her as it initially had to him, Mike started to explain, "That's the name of the—"

"Movie star, yes, I know," Sam interjected with a nod.

"You know?" Mike questioned, surprised. Not that he'd ever been anything remotely resembling a movie buff, knowing the names of only the biggest stars, and then, less than a handful of those, but from what he'd heard, this particular former actress had never been considered to be a performer of any sort of consequence outside her own family.

Sam nodded in response to his question. Somewhere in the distance, a barn owl asked the eternal question. She smiled, thinking the bird's "Who?" co-incided with her conversation with Mike.

"The one constant thing whenever we moved around was our portable TV—the kind with rabbit ears," she specified.

"Rabbit ears?" he questioned, confused.

"Antenna," she explained. "We never had cable anything, even after it was popular. I'd set the TV up first thing whenever we moved into a new apartment and then watched whatever was on. At night, I used to put on old movies to keep me company. The TV's warm blue glow and whatever program was on with the characters talking to each other filled up the silence in the apartment."

"Where was your mom?" Mike asked. As a kid, once his siblings began coming along, causing his mother to be busier and busier, caring for the lot of them, he would have killed for some peace and quiet. The grass was always greener, he thought philosophically.

"Working," Sam answered. "The kind of jobs she got didn't pay all that much, but the bill collectors didn't care. They still wanted to get paid." At times, it was hard to believe she'd been that kid. All this felt as if it had happened to someone else eons ago. "I spent a lot of time alone, which meant I spent a lot of time watching TV and I saw a *lot* of old movies."

She sounded cheerful as she told him about it, but it wasn't hard to read between the lines. "Must have been rough for you."

Sam shrugged away his assessment. "People had it rougher. They still do. And I can't complain. I survived and made something of myself. That lifestyle probably made me tougher," she theorized, then stopped abruptly as her conversation replayed itself in her head. "Hey, wait, how did we start talking about me when I was talking about your father?"

Mike smiled even as he moved his wide shoulders in a vague, careless shrug.

"Guess my dad's not the only one who can turn the tables on people." That he had turned it on her was a source of pride for him, Mike thought. For a brief moment, his eyes met hers. "Apple doesn't fall far from the tree?" he hazarded a guess.

Sam could only stare at him, clearly stunned. "Wow."

"Wow?" he questioned. She nodded in response. "Why 'wow'?" he asked.

"Because you would be the last person in the whole world I would have guessed capable of uttering that kind of a cliché," she told him.

Mike shrugged innocently. "Maybe present company's rubbing off on me," he told her.

"Are you saying I'm clichéd?"

The way she said it sounded like an insult. He hadn't meant it that way. It just seemed like an obvious fact to him, but he kept that to himself.

"Let's just say you're pretty adept at turning a well-used phrase," Mike suggested.

"Is that another term for 'hackneyed'?" she asked.

"No. Hackneyed means trite and well-worn, and you're neither. Especially not the last word," he added under his breath.

Even though he'd turned his head away, she heard him.

Sam felt her mouth curving. She couldn't help it.

Even with his customary gruff manner, Mike made her feel like smiling and when he was friendly like this, he made her willing to do almost anything to keep him this way.

Because "this way" made her pulse race and her heart rate hit new highs.

So what? Jogging has the same effect on you and you don't run the risk of being disappointed in the end. Exasperated with herself, Sam pushed the thought away.

"What?" Mike asked out of the blue.

Since she hadn't said anything, Sam could only stare at him.

"What-what?" she asked.

"You were staring at me, so I thought that maybe something had occurred to you—or I had some of the mashed potato on my lips."

"What you had on your lips was a smile," she told him.

"Yeah, so? What's your point?" He didn't understand where this was going.

"My 'point' is that you should do that more often. Smile," she emphasized in case he wasn't following what she was saying. "Your whole face seems to soften when you smile."

He looked at her somewhat doubtfully. "And that's a good thing?" he asked.

"That's a very good thing," Sam assured him with feeling.

She could feel desire stirring within her, longings that she'd thought she'd buried along with her husband. Apparently they didn't stay buried.

Mike inclined his head. "I'll keep that in mind,"

he told her. "Listen, let me know when you want to go in. No point in you camping out here—unless you want to," he interjected in a voice that told her he was highly skeptical of the latter scenario.

"Same goes for you," she told him.

"I don't understand. What goes for me?"

"I'm very capable of walking around by myself out here," Sam pointed out. It wasn't as though she was taking a walk in a dangerous place and needed his protection. "You don't have to stay with me. I'm sure you've got things you'd rather be doing."

He would have thought that himself—except that he didn't have anything he would have rather been doing than spending this time with her.

"Offhand, can't think of any," he said casually. "Besides, 'capable' though you are," he said and for once his words weren't shrink-wrapped in sarcasm, "it's just too easy to get lost around here in the dark. People who were born here have done it. Strangers are a lot more prone to getting lost than you think," he assured her. "And it's not just here in Texas, if that's what you're thinking. Every year," he went on to illustrate his point, "hikers all over the country go missing because they took a wrong turn, or lost track of the trail, or stayed out after dark. Things always look a whole lot different in the dark than they do in the light," he said simply.

"I'm not hiking, I'm strolling." And this wasn't off the beaten path but, for all intents and purposes, in Mike's own backyard.

"And that's supposed to make a difference?" he asked her.

It did, but she knew he meant well and in light of

all the latent feelings he'd reawakened within her, she let a potential difference of opinion drop by agreeing, "I suppose not."

Sam paused for a moment, debating between continuing out here a little while longer and turning back to go in. The air was crisp with the definite smell of fall, but it wasn't cold, just reasonably cool. All in all, it was close to perfect.

"Your dad's right," she told him, "it is beautiful out here."

"I guess it is," he agreed quietly, except that he wasn't looking up at the sky and the outlying area the way she was. When she glanced in his direction, she saw that he was looking at her.

Sam felt a very strong blush taking hold of her, beginning at her toes and working its way right up to the roots of her hair at lightning speed. She was grateful for the darkness.

The smile on his lips really hadn't abated since they had left the house and now it grew a little more intense. "I'll be sure to tell him you said so," he finally said to her. "He'll undoubtedly take personal credit for making it that way, even though we know he didn't." Again, he was looking directly at her.

His thoughts remained hidden and she had no way of knowing that Mike was fighting the very real urge to take her into his arms and kiss her again, the way he had in the study.

But there was one very large difference.

When he'd kissed her in the study, that had been on an impulse that germinated and flowered. What he was feeling now wasn't so much an impulse as a need.

A need that shimmered between them for a very

long, tempting moment—until he cleared his throat and said, "It's getting kind of windy out here. That sweater you have on—" he nodded toward the one his father had handed her as he all but pushed her out the back door "—isn't going to do much to protect you if it gets any colder than it is now."

She tugged it a little more tightly around her shoulders. "Is that your subtle way of getting me to go in?"

The shrug was careless. "Don't know about subtle, but the going in part sounds about right."

Sam rotated her shoulders a little, fighting off a kink that threatened to set in, bringing an uncomfortable ache with it.

"Maybe you're right."

Mike's lips curved a little more as he said, "I usually am."

Definitely no failure for his ego to thrive, Sam thought, but the observation was laced with humor rather than annoyance. "At the risk of possibly making you utterly impossible to live with, I think I'll go in now."

"Wise choice," he told her, lightly pressing his fingertips to the small of her back as he ushered her in the right direction. "And, contrary to what some of my brothers might say, I've never been impossible to live with."

She caught the narrow differentiation. "Your brothers, not your sister?"

"Alma always thought I could do no wrong," he told her with a straight face that she'd decided could only be arrived at with painstaking practice.

"And if I asked, would she verify what you just said?"

"Sure," he told her. "But maybe you'd better not. Why bother her with trivial matters? Especially at this time of her life, with the pregnancy and all?"

This time she was the one with the grin and it filtered up into her eyes, which he noted seemed to light up.

"I didn't think so."

They were back at the door. The lights had been dimmed and she assumed that Miguel had either turned in or was in the family room, dozing before the big screen TV that his children had bought him for his last birthday. Ray, she guessed, had probably gone to town to see which girl he'd spend the next few hours with.

Which meant that for now, they were technically alone.

Temptation undulated through her, completely surprising Sam. She wasn't the type to think this way, or feel this way. And yet, here she was, thinking and feeling *just* this way.

Make a clean break and get out while you can, a voice in her head urged. But still she remained just where she was, at the back entrance.

Hesitating.

She turned toward Mike and murmured, "Thanks for keeping me company."

"Don't mention it. I did it for selfish reasons."

"Oh?" Was he actually going to say he had feelings for her? Sam highly doubted it. She waited to hear what he was going to come up with.

"Yeah. I didn't want to spend my time being part of the search party looking for you in the morning."

He was quick, she'd grant him that, Sam thought. "Looks like you were spared," she said. Pulling open the door, she turned toward him for a moment, said, "Thanks again," and brushed a very quick kiss against his cheek before swiftly moving out of his reach and out of the back area.

Two minutes later, her heart pounding, she'd made it up the stairs and to her bedroom.

Her lips tingled from the feel and taste of his skin. It seemed to her that they tingled for a long time.

SLEEP STUBBORNLY ELUDED her despite the fact that she had gone to bed shortly after getting back from her walk. After all but rumpling the sheets with her tossing and turning, Sam decided to give up trying to fall asleep for a while.

She felt tired, but at the same time, as if an old-fashioned clock had been wound up to its limit, its coil so tight that it threatened to spring right out of its housing and go shooting across a long space.

This was all Mike's fault.

And a little bit hers, she finally admitted.

Didn't matter whose fault it was. She needed to make the best of the situation and utilize her time well.

Thinking that, she reached for another one of the diaries, the one she'd brought into her room and left on her nightstand. It was one of the books she hadn't gotten a chance to peruse at all yet.

No time like the present.

Reading had put her to sleep once tonight, maybe it could do that again. This time, though, there was no danger of her falling asleep on top of it.

Propping up the pillow behind her, she sat up in the bed and began reading from the beginning of the journal.

My heart aches and I do not know how I am to go on any longer. Robert was the light of my life and now that light has been extinguished. I wanted to marry him when I was old enough. I think he had wanted it, too. But now it will never be possible. How can I continue when my heart has no reason to go on beating?

And yet, there is something inside of me that will not let me give up, will not let me just die quietly. Something that will not allow those terrible killers of my beloved Robert to win. I will survive despite what they will do to me and with me. I will survive so that Robert will not be forgotten. His will be the name on my lips when I am rescued. And I will be rescued.

THE WORD *WILL* was underlined at least five times. So much so that the page just beneath the word was actually slightly torn from the sheer pressure of the underlining.

Sam sighed. As from the very beginning, she found herself silently rooting for Marguerite to triumph over her captors.

She read a little more and doing so had the desired effect. She was getting sleepy.

Finally.

As her eyelids began to feel heavier and heavier, Sam laid the volume down beside her bed. No doubt about it, this woman who'd lived all those years ago had been strong and exceedingly admirable. Miguel would be proud to be related to her, proud to have her be a part of his family tree.

This was going to be a really good story to pass on to his grandchildren. She wouldn't rest until she'd turned all these diaries into the very best memoir that she could. In addition, she decided, the originals should be carefully preserved and placed in a vault so that these same grandchildren and future grandchildren would be able to access them and read them for themselves.

This was a really wonderful project and she was very glad that she could be a part of it.

It seemed that the moment her eyes were closed and her mind released its grip on her thoughts, she began to dream. And in her dream, she was reliving everything that she had just read in the diary.

She literally felt the ache that Marguerite felt over losing Robert.

Except that the face of Robert did not belong to the man who had lived so long ago and had been so vividly described in another one of Marguerite's journals. Neither did that face belong to Danny, the way she would have thought it logically would, since he had been her love the way Marguerite had thought of Robert.

When she felt the ache of loss, the face of the man she was remembering belonged to Mike.

Sam woke up abruptly in a cold sweat just as dawn peeled away the darkness outside her window.

Chapter Twelve

Sam was hesitant about venturing downstairs for breakfast. So much so that she deliberately took her time in getting dressed and ready, knowing that mornings on the ranch began early and if she was slow enough, the men would finish their breakfast and leave before she came to the table.

She was counting on that.

Ordinarily, she looked forward to the interaction she both witnessed and took part in. She truly enjoyed the conversation—as well as the grunting—that went on around her. It made her feel, for a little while, that she was included. That the life she had always longed for in her daydreams, being in a family, had suddenly materialized—even though she was well aware that it hadn't, that once this project she was working on was completed, she would return to her solitary existence and these people she'd come to like so much would go on with theirs.

Eventually—most likely sooner than later—her presence here would be forgotten.

But this morning was different from the other mornings. This morning she was still very vividly aware of the sexual reaction she'd had to Mike in her dreams. Unable to keep her guard up while asleep, her mind was free to extrapolate on the feelings she was attempting to smother. Feelings that had been brought to the foreground when he'd kissed her in the study.

Feelings that were even now growing.

Feelings for Mike.

She was afraid he'd see that in her eyes, in her very expression. She wasn't much of an actress and it was better not to risk exposure just for the momentary thrill of experiencing another family breakfast.

And yet, like the proverbial moth that couldn't resist the seductive allure of the flame, Sam found herself making her way downstairs, drawn to the voices coming from the dining room.

Miguel was not the first to see her. Mike was. His father must have noted the direction his oldest was looking and saw that their houseguest was finally entering the room.

Picking up his napkin from his lap, Miguel half rose in his seat and was the first to greet her.

As always, his smile was warm, welcoming. And— was that her imagination?—a little wider this morning.

"Good morning, Samantha," he called out in his booming voice. "I hope you slept well."

As long as she could remain vague, she could be honest, Sam decided. "Off and on, actually."

Miguel looked at her for a moment before going on to express his concern. "Is there anything I can do?" But the way he asked gave her the impression that he didn't believe that there was.

Or that he was the reason for her sleeplessness.

She was being paranoid, Sam thought, upbraiding herself.

In response to Miguel's polite question, Sam shook her head. "Maybe you were right," she allowed, grasping at the first excuse she could think of. "Maybe I've been working on the project too hard."

"I am glad to hear you say that," Miguel told her.

She raised her eyes to his, wondering if perhaps they'd hit a language problem. But before she could try to correct him, the next thing he said explained his feelings more clearly.

"I was going to suggest that you accompany Miguel into town today, perhaps stop by at Miss Joan's. She is asking about you and I thought, as you writers always say, a picture is worth a thousand words, so how much more is the actually living, breathing person worth?"

"You planning on selling Sam, Dad?" Ray asked wryly, glancing in his direction.

"Of course not," Miguel answered indignantly, looking appalled at the very suggestion. Then he directed his soft brown eyes toward his guest. "See what I have to put up with? They like to play their little word games and corner me whenever they can because they think they are so much more clever than an old man." His smile grew and his eyes crinkled as he looked at her. "You are a breath of fresh air compared to these two."

"If I'm such a breath of fresh air, why are you sending me off to town?" she asked, amused despite herself.

"I am sending you to town because you have been stuck in that study with the dust of the past far too long. A good balance between work and enjoying yourself is necessary for a healthy mind," he told her, sounding as if he wholeheartedly believed this philosophy.

"And just how is making her go to town with Mike going to keep her mind healthy?" Ray asked as he took a second helping of everything—sausages, eggs, pancakes—onto his plate. "If you ask me, it'll do just the opposite."

"But I was not asking you, was I?" Miguel pointed out.

"Maybe you and I should go into town, Miguel," Sam suggested.

She knew she'd feel a lot more at ease if it was the older man she was traveling with, not his son. Just looking at Mike this morning had her thoughts scattering like so many dandelions caught up in a strong spring breeze.

"Ah, if only I could," Miguel lamented with a deep, heartfelt sigh. "But I'm afraid that I am going to be very busy."

In between bites, Ray fixed his father with a quizzical look. "Doing what?"

"Busy things," Miguel informed his youngest tersely, clearly not prepared to elaborate at this moment just what that involved.

"That's why he asked me to go to town in the first place," Mike told her, finally speaking up.

He knew his father was up to something and knew, too, that begging off, making things difficult, or bedeviling his father with questions as to why things had to go this particular route was *not* the way to go. When his father got a notion into his head, nothing short of a burning bush on the front porch would dissuade the man from pursuing that notion.

"If you'd like to come along," Mike continued telling her, "I'll be leaving in about half an hour."

Okay, she thought, this was where she begged off, saying that she was making a breakthrough in the journals, or that she was coming down with something and didn't want to risk giving this "something" to him or his family. This was the exact moment for her to say, "Thanks but no thanks," perhaps even adding "Maybe next time" so that she didn't sound rude.

So just how did the word *Okay,* escape her lips instead?

But it did. She heard it, as did Miguel and his two sons.

She'd obviously betrayed herself. There was no hope for her, not if she couldn't even rely on herself.

She was just doing it to prove to herself that it was ridiculous to allow a dream—a completely baseless, harmless dream—to intimidate her. People had strange dreams all the time, they didn't spend their lives cowering in closets or under beds after they've had them. After all, life went on.

SAM CLUNG TO her silence for the first few minutes into the trip to Forever. But the quiet in the cab of the truck made her edgy and she knew Mike was not about to just break into conversation—at least not unless she gave him something to work with. The man in the driver's seat beside her was many things, she'd come to realize, but when it came to talking, he really wasn't a self-starter.

Knotting her fingers together in her lap, Sam took

the plunge and asked, "Does your father always take such an active interest in people's social lives?" When Mike gave her a look, she added, "Most of the other people I've worked with didn't really express any kind of concern about whether I was eating enough or getting in enough 'night air' and they definitely didn't care one way or the other about whether I was socializing enough while I was engaged in collaborating on their autobiographies. The project was the main thing—the *only* thing," she emphasized, "not whether or not I got out and mingled with people."

Mike's broad shoulders rose and fell in a careless shrug. "Dad's different—or at least he is now," he qualified. He was looking straight ahead at the road, but his mind had taken a brief detour and slipped back into the past. "When Mom was alive, all he cared about was providing for her and for us. It seemed like he was always working back then, training the horses, doing the work of three men and eating like half the person he was. His health suffered, but he didn't pay attention. He just plowed ahead.

"He missed a lot of family milestones because he was always so busy," Mike recalled. Recalled, too, resenting his father for that on more than one occasion. "It took Mom getting sick for him to suddenly take stock of things and realize what was really important in life. Realize how much he'd missed."

The memories Mike was summoning hurt, but he couldn't turn his back on them and stop talking.

"I heard him tell Mom that he would have given ten years of his life just to gain back a little of what he'd lost. Instead, he lost Mom," he said quietly, still staring at the road. "That really drove the message home to him. He's been a changed man ever since then. It's kind of like he's not just living for himself but for Mom, as well," Mike theorized. "And it's also made him extra sensitive to other people's omissions and faults." Getting his emotions under control again, Mike finally spared her a glance. "Like you working too much."

Except, the way she saw it, there was a difference here. "He's *paying* me to work."

Mike inclined his head, not quite conceding the point to her. "It's his money, which means he can pay for what he wants and if he wants you to go to town instead of spend that time working, well, I'm guessing he's entitled to feel he should have you go to town because he's willing to pay for that, too."

She rolled the argument over in her head. She supposed, in a strange sort of way, Mike was right. Which made this the most unusual work situation she had ever been in.

"Your father is a very strange man," she told Mike.

"You'll get no argument from me," Mike told her with a dry laugh. "But at the same time, he's also a very unique man."

Now she was the one who couldn't argue with the point that was being made.

Sam nodded. "That, too."

She couldn't help thinking that it seemed to her that the "unique man" was also throwing Mike and her together a great deal.

Was that just by accident, or was he doing it deliberately?

The next minute, Sam chided herself for allowing her imagination, its flames fanned high by last night's dream, to get the better of her. Miguel Rodriguez was not setting her up with his son, he was just making sure she was looked after, that was all, Sam thought as the diner came into view.

She felt the truck begin to slow down. "We're stopping here first?"

"Might as well. If Miss Joan hears that I brought you to town and she wasn't first on my list—well, it wouldn't be a pretty sight, trust me," Mike assured her with a perfectly somber expression. She had no idea if he was putting her on.

Pulling in at an angle in order to claim a bit of space for his truck, Mike parked the vehicle then climbed out. He waited a moment for Sam to emerge, then led the way up the diner's front steps.

As expected, Miss Joan was behind the counter, talking to someone as she poured another one of the diner's regulars his second cup of coffee.

The woman raised her eyes from the cup when she heard the front door open. She finished topping off the man's coffee without spilling a drop.

If she was surprised to see Sam, she gave no indication. From all signs, this was just a typical weekday morning for the woman.

"Sit yourselves down," she called out, promising Sam and Mike, "I'll be with you in a minute."

"You want a table or the counter?" Mike asked.

Sam was undecided for a moment, clearly favoring selecting a table because it afforded privacy, something she knew they both desired. But then she decided that in this case, privacy wasn't why they had come here to begin with.

"The counter," Sam told him. "If we sit at the counter, Miss Joan won't have that far to go."

Since he'd stopped here first because his father had asked him to, due to Miss Joan's inquiries after Sam, sitting at the counter was fine with him. But he decided to bait Sam a little.

"What does distance have to do with it?" he asked.

"It's not the distance so much as the act of walking," she told him. "Miss Joan's probably on her feet for most of the day. The less she has to walk, the less she hurts."

It took him a moment to digest Sam's reasoning. When he did, something else became clear to him, as well.

"Your mom was a waitress." It was an educated guess on his part.

Sam nodded. "In one of her many jobs," she replied. Her mouth curved a little as she recalled, "I got to massage her feet a lot when I was a kid."

That was what she remembered most about her mother. Sitting on the sofa, watching some program that made her mother laugh—she couldn't remember the name—and massaging her mother's aching feet. It was the closest they'd come to having real conversations. Her mother would tell her that she had gifted hands and often her mother would sigh with contentment after the first half hour had passed. It was around that point that her mother would tell her that her massaging had succeeded in making her feel human again.

But obviously Tony made her feel something more than that because it was Tony her mother took off with, leaving only a note in her wake saying that she was eighteen now and old enough to take care of herself. After all, she went on to write, she'd been sixteen herself when she'd had her and they had made a go of it, hadn't they? Now it was time for her to either go her own way, or follow in her mother's footsteps, but either way, she had to do it alone.

She had read that note over and over again in disbelief. She read it until her eyes hurt. The words never changed. The message remained the same.

Lost in momentary thought, she didn't realize that Mike was now watching her expectantly. He'd said something and was waiting for her to answer.

Did she pretend to think it over and try to wing it, or did she admit to being preoccupied and ask him to repeat what he'd said?

She wound up having to do neither because he repeated himself without being prompted.

"Well? Are you going to sit down at the counter, or are you waiting for a personal, engraved invitation?" Mike asked.

She realized that she was still standing beside the stool. "I guess I'll sit." She smiled with a little amusement as she glanced at him. "The other way might be too long a wait."

"So you *can* answer back," Miss Joan noted as she moved to their end of the counter, the ever-present pot of coffee in her hand, ready for her to pour at a moment's notice. "Good for you, girl. Now you've just got to work on your sarcasm."

"She's doing just fine, Miss Joan," Mike assured her. "She doesn't need any more encouragement, especially not from an expert like you."

Miss Joan snorted, filling up first her cup, then his before retiring the pot to its rightful place in front of the urn.

"Flattery's not going to get you anywhere, boy," she told him. "And as for what you just said about her doing just fine, hell, that's a surefire way to know that she's not, if you're praising her for her 'talent,'" Miss Joan said, her eyes deliberately shifting toward the newest young lady at her counter. "But you look none the worse for wear, sugar, so I guess you're either holding your own—or Miguel and the boys're not picking on you much." Miss Joan closed one eye slightly as she fixed her with a penetrating look. "Which is it?"

"Miguel and Ray have been nothing but gentlemen," she told Miss Joan.

"A gentleman?" Mike hooted. "Did you *see* the way Ray looks at you? Like you're a double-decker sandwich and he hasn't eaten in a week."

Both women chose to ignore what Mike was saying at this point. "And him?" Miss Joan asked, nodding at Mike.

Sam trod lightly, not wanting Mike to get the wrong impression and think that she was either giving him a pass or worse, had feelings for him. She wanted him to think that things were just casual between them and that being with him didn't instantly weaken her kneecaps.

"He's what we call a work in progress," Sam finally said.

The response apparently really tickled Miss Joan

and she had no qualms about owning up to it by laughing.

Mike looked less than pleased at the woman's reaction.

Chapter Thirteen

"Okay, what's next?" Sam asked when she and Mike finally walked out of the diner.

In his estimation, what had begun as a quick pit stop had turned into one long "getting-reacquainted-stop" instead that had eaten away an hour rather than the ten to fifteen minutes he'd initially assumed it would take. He had discovered, much to his embarrassment, that he'd underestimated how far Miss Joan was inclined to delve when she asked questions in an effort to get to know Sam "better."

While this took the pressure away from him when it came to having to make conversation, it also severely impeded his timetable.

Mike got into the truck before he bit off an answer to her question. "Need to stop at the feed store to get some feed—"

"Novel concept," she commented brightly. "Feed at a feed store."

He shot her a dark look as he started up the truck. "And then the emporium."

"What are we getting there?" Sam asked.

The question was no sooner out of her mouth than she realized how presumptive that sounded. *They* weren't getting anything except in the absolute definition of the word since they were both going to the emporium together, But Mike was shopping according to his father's list and anything he bought was meant for his family and didn't involve her. She was just incidental in the process, being along for the ride, nothing more.

"I mean what are you getting there?" she corrected herself.

The abrupt rephrasing wasn't lost on him. Was that her way of saying she was trying to distance herself from him as well as his family? Telling himself that was a good thing, something he wanted, somehow just didn't seem to quell the odd restlessness he felt now and had been feeling for the better part of the past month.

Mike forced himself to focus on the bare bones of her question and nothing more as he drove away from Miss Joan's diner to the next stop on his list.

"Dad asked me to buy the turkey for next week and bring it as well as a few other things home," he told her. As he said it, he decided that maybe the emporium should be his next stop rather than the feed store. He had a lot more to buy at the former.

Sam looked at him in surprise. "You're *buying* a turkey?" she questioned.

"Have to," he told her dryly. "The sheriff frowns on stealing it and besides, I'm not exactly wearing the right kind of jacket to get away with smuggling it out of the store."

Sam shook her head. "No, I mean you're buying it instead of shooting it?"

"Don't have to," he told her, turning down the next street. "It's already dead."

She rolled her eyes. "What I meant was that I was afraid you were going to hunt your own turkey and bring it down."

Well, at least there they were in agreement, he thought. "I don't like killing things," he told Sam simply.

Sam frowned. "But didn't you say you went hunting?"

"Yeah, that's because I do once in a while." And then it dawned on him. Mike saw her problem. A hint of a smile curved his lips as he cleared up the misunderstanding. "Hunting doesn't mean killing."

"What does it mean?" she asked Mike uncertainly.

"Hunting," he answered. Then, because Sam still looked as confused as she had a minute ago, he elaborated. "I like the challenge of hunting something, of tracking it down. Animals are cunning in their own unique way," he said with respect. "I like pitting myself against them. That doesn't mean I like killing them. I don't have to kill some living creature to be the 'winner' or prove something. I don't like killing," he told her flatly again.

Mike made the statement with such feeling, she looked up at him. "You sound as if you've done it."

There was no point in denying it. He'd done it and it hadn't increased his love of the kill. On the contrary, it had made him even more against it. "I did."

"What did you kill?" she pressed, instinctively aware that if she didn't press him, Mike wasn't going to say another word on the subject.

"A mountain lion," he finally said. "I had to. It was

coming right at me and at that point, he left me no choice. I couldn't outrun him. It was either the mountain lion, or me."

"I'm glad you picked you." The words tumbled out of Sam's mouth before she had a chance to think it through.

Her remark, uttered spontaneously, surprised him. Mike spared her a look. "Mind if I ask why?"

Sam fell back on the family dynamics as an excuse for saying what she had. "I think losing you would have broken your father's heart."

Mike shrugged off the suggestion. It wasn't as if he was his father's only child, or even his only son. "He's got spares."

Her eyes widened as she regarded his rigid profile.

"I've met all of you. You're definitely not interchangeable," Sam assured him. Because he didn't like to seek animals out and kill them, she cut him a little slack regarding the philosophy he'd just spouted. "And your dad loves each one of you—that means you, too. It's not like taking one toy boat out of a bathtub filled with them. The water doesn't rush in to fill the void, causing the other boats to move in closer. Life's not like that—nor should it be," she informed him with feeling.

Mike laughed shortly. "Easy to see you make your living with words."

"Just part of my living," she corrected. "The rest I make by observing people—closely," she emphasized.

Sam had a hunch that she wasn't going to convince this man of anything today. For now, he'd made up his mind and getting him to see things her way was like trying to turn a cast-iron stove around using one hand—it just wasn't possible.

"So, how big a turkey are you looking to get?" she asked him breezily.

He didn't have to look at the list in his breast pocket to remember his father's specifications. "Seeing as how it'll be feeding sixteen people or so, I'd say I'm looking for the biggest one they've got. Maybe in the neighborhood of thirty-two pounds," he estimated. Even Alma ate like she'd been starved for a week when it came to the turkey and stuffing at Thanksgiving. And this year, his sister would be eating for two. He might have to get her a turkey of her own, he mused.

"What if you don't find one that big?"

That was simple enough. "Then I bring home two," he told her. "The freezer we have in the storeroom is big enough to hold a full-sized man—it sure as hell can hold a couple of Thanksgiving turkeys for a week," he assured her.

"And you really don't bag your own?" she asked, watching his face closely.

"You looking for me to bring back a signed sworn statement from a turkey that I never took a shot at it?" he deadpanned, aware, even though he wasn't looking at her, that she was studying him very carefully. Sam was watching him so hard, he was surprised her eyes weren't leaving marks on his skin.

"No, it just seemed like something you'd do around here," she explained.

"Maybe someone else does it," he granted, "but not me. Besides, you ever have to clean a bird?" he asked her out of the blue. "I mean *really* clean a bird?" Sam moved her head from side to side in response to his question. The very thought made her consider giving up meat—at least for a moment. "Those feathers don't just fall off in surrender once the bird's drawn his last breath. They go right on clinging to that miserable skin until you pluck them out—one by one. Trust me, that amounts to a hell of a lot of plucking. It's not exactly something I'd like to spend my time doing."

"I don't see you plucking," she agreed. "I see you passing that chore off to someone else."

He came to a stop before one of Forever's four traffic lights. It was red, as was his impatience since there *was* no traffic heading the opposite way.

"Is that it?" he asked.

"Is what it?"

"Is that why you're asking all these questions about whether or not I was going to hunt the family's Thanksgiving turkey? Because you're afraid once I brought it back, I'd make you pluck the feathers off the bird?"

"No," she denied with feeling. "I just don't like the idea of you tracking down and shooting a poor, defenseless bird."

"Defenseless?" He hooted. "Obviously you've never been charged at by an angry turkey," he concluded with a laugh. "They can make you really fear for your life. Those beaks of theirs are vicious. Good thing turkeys can't climb a tree."

"A turkey chase you up a tree?" she asked, unable to keep a straight face. Picturing the scene vividly in her mind had her laughing out loud despite all attempts to remain impassive.

"Not me, Gabe," Mike told her. "Dunno what he

did, but whatever it was, it got this fat old turkey moving like a feathered freight train, charging right at him. Gabe came running by for all that he was worth, but that old bird just kept on coming."

She wasn't sure if he was pulling her leg, but for the sake of argument, she decided to act as if she believed him.

"What happened?"

He shrugged, as if it was a foregone conclusion, given what he'd just said about climbing a tree. "The turkey finally went away."

If the bird was angry enough to charge, she assumed that he would have been angry enough to hang around for a while.

"Just like that?" she questioned.

Mike shrugged again. He didn't like elaborating if it wound up placing any attention on him. And he'd been the one to get the turkey to stop treeing Gabe.

"It took a little doing," he allowed.

"And just what was it you were doing?"

He was beginning to feel that they were too evenly matched—she asked too many questions. "How did you know it was me?"

"Because you're telling the story and you haven't mentioned anyone else being there besides Gabe and the turkey. I doubt if the turkey just changed his mind, shrugged and strolled away. So," she repeated, "what did you do?"

He had a feeling she wasn't going to back off until he told her. Might as well not draw this out any longer than it already was.

"I tossed a few well-aimed rocks his way—just enough to sting," he told her.

That implied an awful lot of knowledge on his part, she thought. "And you'd know just how much that would be?"

To which he grinned. Not smiled, grinned, she noted. Like her question amused him. She wasn't altogether sure she liked that.

"I'm a country boy," he told her. "That kind of thing is second nature to us."

"Kind of like God saying you'll never get to drive a flaming red Ferrari, but you'll know how big a rock to use to make a turkey feel a sting?"

"Yeah, kind of like that," he granted, playing along. Without realizing it, he'd completely passed by the feed store and had gone on to the emporium.

Mike quickly pulled up into the first empty space he saw before he passed by this, too, and had to circle around to get back here.

Getting out, he told her, "You can stay in the truck if you want."

Even as he said it, he had a feeling that she wasn't about to stay put.

And he was right. The next moment, Sam was jumping down from her seat. "And miss out looking for a thirty-two-pound turkey? I don't think so."

Okay, he'd play along, Mike thought. The boards creaked beneath his feet as he went up the steps leading into the emporium.

"Doesn't take much to entertain you, does it?" he quipped.

She had no idea why, but the question took her back to yesterday evening in the study. To the unexpected kiss that lit up her very blood and how it all but set fire to her veins.

"No," she said softly, walking through the door he held open for her, "it doesn't."

"WHAT DID YOU BUY?" Miguel asked, stunned as he stared at the multiple grocery bags that his son had brought in and was still bringing in.

The kitchen table, which was more of a work area than a place where they ate their morning meal, was completely covered with bags. There were grocery bags on the chairs and on the floor, as well. From the looks of it, most were filled to capacity.

"I gave you a list," Miguel called after his son as Mike went back to the truck for one last trip. "This looks like you bought out the store." The last time something like this happened, it was because there were flash flood storm warnings and they had stocked up on supplies. But the forecast for the next week was for clear skies. "You know something I don't?" he asked.

"Don't look at me," Mike protested, coming in with the last load. Both his arms were filled. He set these bags down on the floor, as well. "This was her idea." He nodded toward Sam.

Miguel looked quizzically at his houseguest. "It was your idea to clean out the emporium?"

"Don't worry, I paid for the groceries I bought," she assured him. Sam was fairly bubbling with excitement as she thought about taking part in the upcoming Thanksgiving celebration.

"I was not worried about who paid for it, I am just wondering what all this is for—and where we are going to put it," Miguel told her.

"Well, since you're having so many people here for

Thanksgiving," Sam answered, "hopefully, this'll all be going into their stomachs within the week."

Mike cleared off one chair and wearily sank down in it for a couple of minutes. When Sam had gotten going, it seemed like there was no stopping her. He found himself hurrying after her with the grocery cart and barely keeping up. She might have been shorter than he was, but she moved a hell of a lot faster when she wanted to.

"You realize you're supposed to stuff the turkey, not the people, at Thanksgiving," Mike pointed out.

She was about to answer him when Rosa came in. The moment the older woman saw the grocery bags all over her kitchen, a stunned squeal escaped her voice as, her hands on hips, the housekeeper cried, "What have you done to my poor kitchen? Why are all these bags here? Are we having a charity drive?"

"Don't worry, Rosa, I'll put everything away," Sam assured the other woman. Then she turned back to Miguel and continued with her explanation. "I thought, since you were having all these people here and you were nice enough to invite me, too, that I'd bake a few things, make a few side dishes, things like that," she told him, her eyes shining. "I like to cook," she added, "but there's never anyone to cook for but me and it seems like a huge waste to go through all that trouble for just one person," she said quietly. Alone, she tended to eat uninspired meals over the sink. She was really looking forward to next week.

Her voice picked up, sounding eager again as she said, "I hope you don't mind." With that, she swiftly swung around to say the very same thing to Rosa, well aware that it might have technically been Miguel's kitchen, but Rosa was the one who ruled over it.

Rosa responded first before her employer. "Well, if Mr. Miguel doesn't mind, I would certainly not mind the help," Rosa told her.

It was obvious to the others that the housekeeper was more than won over by this enthusiastic little blonde collaborator and was only being slow to agree because Rosa felt she was supposed to hold out a little.

"I do not mind," Miguel told his housekeeper, then turned to look at Sam. "But I do not want you to feel that you have to do all this for some reason." he said to Sam. "Because you do not. Besides, my daughter and daughters-in-law are all coming early to help Rosa prepare the evening meal."

"I know I don't 'have' to," Sam answered. "But I really want to." Her smile was wide and sunny as she continued taking the groceries into the storeroom where she intended to unpack them. "How do you want this arranged?" she asked Rosa, nodding at the bags she was holding. "By size, by type or maybe alphabetically?"

In response, Rosa took the two bags Sam was holding. She put them back on the table, then dramatically took one of Sam's now empty hands and connected that hand to one of Mike's.

"Do something with her," she ordered Mike, then informed everyone in the room, "I will take care of the unpacking and the putting away."

With that, the diminutive housekeeper picked up the two grocery bags she'd put on the table and marched into the storage room.

The sound of Miguel's wholehearted laughter followed her out. The set of her shoulders told everyone who was watching that despite her seemingly gruff manner, the housekeeper was indeed smiling.

Perhaps even grinning.

The young woman who was his houseguest seemed to have that sort of effect on people, Miguel noted.

Chapter Fourteen

Sam was up before dawn even had a chance to send faint shafts of light peering in through her window.

It was Thanksgiving morning and she had a lot to do.

The very thought that she did had her grinning broadly to herself. It felt good to be involved, to have a list of tasks to do for people she had come to care about a great deal.

Even though she was up and ready before six, Sam didn't stop for breakfast. There was no time to linger over a meal. She did, however, stick her head into the dining room every so often to see if Mike, Ray and their father had finished eating. She explained that she needed to commandeer the room. She refused to tell any of them why, but requested that they stay clear of the room until it was time for dinner—which was a good ten hours away by Mike's reckoning.

Mike had shrugged his shoulders, told himself that whatever she was up to was her business and after finishing his breakfast, he had gone about his chores as usual. After all, horses and cattle didn't quietly vanish just because it was Thanksgiving or Christmas or any other holiday for that matter. They needed to be fed and tended to 365 days a year without fail.

But around noon, when his rumbling stomach usually made him pause to have some sort of lunch no matter if he was at home or on the open range, Mike's curiosity finally got the better of him.

It wasn't so much about what was going on in the dining room as it was about what the person who was implementing all this secrecy was doing.

Just exactly what was Sam up to that she didn't want any of them to see?

Prepared with an excuse if she suddenly began questioning his "barging" into the the kitchen, Mike made his way there.

From the sound of it as he approached, he would have said that the recently expanded room had become the hub of activity today. There was far more noise coming from the kitchen than he would have guessed that two women could possibly make without something like a vintage 1967 Camaro being involved.

The heat from the oven was the first thing he became aware of as he ventured into the kitchen.

Rosa had the oven door open and she had slid the huge turkey out just enough to make basting easier for her. Especially since Angel, Gabe's wife and Miss Joan's chief cook, had apparently arrived early and was now in the midst of helping her prepare the main course.

The turkey seemed to fill up the entire opening.

Just as he walked in, Rosa looked up and Angel turned to look over her shoulder.

Rosa was smiling as she nodded her approval. Not of him, but of the turkey he had purchased and brought home. Everyone agreed that it had to be the largest turkey in the county, possibly several counties. More importantly, it was guaranteed to feed everyone in his family three times over. There would be plenty for leftovers to send home with various family members when they left the ranch late tonight.

The kitchen was a cauldron of warm, tempting scents and smells all blending together so that it was difficult for him to separate them—not that he really saw any need to do that. The combined aroma was an absolute feast for his senses.

"Looks like you've outdone yourself again, Rosa, Angel," he said, complimenting the two women.

"It goes faster—and better—when I have help," Rosa qualified, nodding at Angel and then toward the kitchen table.

Sam was standing at the table, patiently rolling something between the palms of her hands, then placing the end product on what looked like a flat piece of metal. He had no idea what she was doing. Usually able to adjust to his surroundings, Mike was *not* at home in a kitchen beyond opening a refrigerator and helping himself to whatever edible thing he found there. How it had become edible was beyond his need to know.

Sam's creation was lined up in three long rows on the metal sheet, which in turn had some kind of paper on it.

Mike moved closer to the table now, his eyes never leaving the woman who seemed completely preoccupied with her work.

"Is being covered from head to foot with flour part of the process?" Mike couldn't resist asking her. Even as he asked, he reached out to brush away some of the flour that had gotten on her cheek.

As if suddenly coming to life, Sam pulled her head back. "If you want to be useful, go talk to your father or your brother."

He didn't understand the connection. "How is that being useful?"

"Well, if you're in there, it'll keep you from hovering over me," she told him.

Because her hair had fallen into her eyes as she nodded toward the kitchen doorway, she tried to push it back with the back of her wrist. Her hands were covered with flour, bits and pieces of ground almonds and dough, all of which she was shaping into tiny balls before she dusted the whole tray with powdered sugar. She then placed the tray into the oven to bake for ten minutes above the roasting turkey.

She didn't succeed in pushing back her hair, but she did get more flour on her forehead and a little rained down on her chest.

"Here, let me at least do that before I'm banished into exile."

He said it so seriously Sam didn't realize he was teasing until she saw the amused glint in his eyes. But then her vision became just a shade blurry when she felt his fingertips skim along her skin as he gently moved the wayward strand of hair back and into submission.

He deliberately left the dusting of flour on her shirt although he was sorely tempted to brush it away.

"Better?" he asked, his voice low and, as far as she was concerned, sexy as hell.

There was a fire inside of her. A fire that had nothing to do with the temporary blast of heat from the oven and everything to do with the man standing over her, making her pulse race with dazed wonder.

She swallowed, feeling shaky. "Even better if you get out of our hair," she told him, the inside of her mouth as dry as the panhandle in the middle of July.

Mike raised his hands in mock surrender. "Already gone," he told her as he edged his way toward the doorway.

Not hardly, Sam couldn't help thinking.

He'd barely crossed the threshold and disappeared from view before Rosa told her quite firmly, "He likes you, that one."

Angel seconded her opinion.

Inhaling at the wrong time because the blatant statement had caught her completely off guard, Sam began coughing. When it looked as if she couldn't stop and Angel's hitting her on the back didn't help, Rosa poured water into a glass and placed it at her elbow on the edge of the table.

"Drink," she ordered rather than encouraged.

Sam almost choked on the water, but then she finally managed to stop coughing and catch her breath. Her eyes had become watery in the process.

"And I see that you like Mr. Mike, as well," Rosa concluded from the display she'd just been privy to. Exchanging glances with Angel, Rosa nodded, satisfied with what she'd seen and with the conclusion she'd drawn from it. "He is a good man, the younger Miguel, just like his father. He was always very quiet, even as a little boy," the housekeeper recalled, returning the turkey to its place inside the oven. It had hours left to go. "But he has not been so quiet this last month." Rosa looked at her and it felt as if the small black eyes were literally penetrating her skin, "I think you are the reason."

Taking a deep breath, Sam deliberately focused on what she was doing. There were still two rows of cookies to form.

"Me?" Sam asked in surprise. She could feel her pulse starting up again. This was making her feel light-headed. "I think you're imagining things, Rosa."

"And I think you are denying things," the petite woman countered. "But if seeing what is in front of your face makes you uncomfortable, then please, go ahead and deny it. But no matter how much you do, it does not make it any less true."

Angel said nothing, but her smile said it all as far as Sam could tell.

Well, there was apparently no winning here, Sam thought. When outmaneuvered, change course—that was her motto.

The next moment, Sam very carefully guided the conversation toward the meal they were working on for tonight and her contribution to it.

One look at Rosa's face told her that the housekeeper knew what she was up to, but for now, the woman had obviously decided to allow her to slide.

Which was just fine with Sam.

All she wanted was to get through the evening without making anyone ill. Just the thought of the dinner this evening had excitement pumping through her veins.

Except for when she was too briefly married to Danny, Sam couldn't remember the last time she'd sat down to a table for the holiday that wasn't set up directly before the portable television set.

Even her marriage to Danny seemed like it had happened in a different lifetime now. Or maybe it had all just taken place in a dream she'd invented.

But today wasn't for negative thoughts, Sam told herself. Today was for celebrating a special holiday with a special family. That was all that mattered. Banishing any and all thoughts that weren't directly connected to the side dishes and desserts she was planning to prepare, Sam threw herself into the work that was right in front of her.

"THIS, THIS IS TRULY beautiful, Samantha," Miguel pronounced, walking into the dining room as he led the rest of his family into the festively decorated room. Armed with colorful decorations she had created out of streamers and crepe paper late last night in her room, Sam had transformed the masculine-looking room into a feast for the eyes. "You have worked too hard. And I feel guilty," the patriarch confessed, raising his voice to be heard above the low-level din that pervaded the first and possibly the second floor of his house. He took his place at the head of the table while his offspring and their other halves seated themselves around the long table. "You are a guest, Samantha, you were not supposed to be working in the hot kitchen, preparing our meals."

"No, that is what he pays me for," Rosa interjected as she walked in carrying a large bowl of baked yams and apples, topped off with a layer of cinnamon sugar.

"I pay you for your winning personality, Rosa. The food is just a bonus," Miguel told the woman who had worked for him ever since he'd brought his young bride here, all those years ago.

The housekeeper made a dismissive noise as she went back into the kitchen. Sam looked after the woman, debating, then rose to her feet, as well.

"You are leaving?" Miguel asked, surprised. "Are you not staying for the meal?"

"Yes, of course," she assured him. "But Rosa needs help," she said, about to make her way back to the kitchen to bring in the various other side dishes made to complement the turkey.

Miguel placed his hand over hers, holding her in place. "And she will have it. Miguel, Gabriel, Raphael, go, help the poor woman," he instructed. "And you, you sit here and rest, along with all the other lovely ladies in my family." He said it with a smile, but Sam had a feeling that he was not about to take no for an answer. So she sat down and pretended that the phrase, "my family" included her, as well. At least for today.

Meanwhile the three sons he had singled out dutifully rose and went to the kitchen. The moment they did, everyone in the dining room could hear the housekeeper attempting to banish them back to the dining room as she ordered, "Get out from under my feet, please!"

Sam could almost hear the woman's clenched teeth.

A moment later, Gabe and Rafe were back, empty-handed, with semi-sheepish expressions on their faces as they passed their father.

"You know what Rosa's like, Dad," Rafe told his father.

Only Mike walked in carrying something and since it was the turkey and too unwieldy for the five-foot-tall housekeeper to manage by herself, Sam understood why Rosa would have relented in this case.

Besides, she was beginning to realize that Mike wasn't like his brothers. He didn't budge if he didn't want to and no amount of coercion could make him. She rather liked that about him.

Mike placed the large, golden roasted bird before his father.

"Dad," he declared, gesturing toward the platter as he backed away, "the next step is yours."

"And here I thought that it was yours," Miguel said to his oldest with an unfathomable smile playing on his lips.

Mike said nothing, sensing that they were no longer talking about the turkey.

"The writer made the stuffing," Rosa informed Miguel as she came in from the kitchen with a huge bowl of stuffing. "She followed words on a piece of paper she carried in her pocket," the woman added by way of a disclaimer.

"It tastes great," Angel told her father-in-law. "I sampled it."

"Samantha?" he asked, turning toward her. "How much *did* you cook today?"

"Just a few things," she said, shrugging off any undue credit. "Rosa and Angel had so much to do, I thought I should pitch in and help," Sam told him.

"Besides the stuffing with all those little meats in them," Rosa said, pointing things out on the table as they were being set down. "She also made cakes of tea for Russians."

Mike looked at the woman sitting next to him,

clearly confused—as were most of the others at the table. "You made what?"

"Russian Tea Cakes," Sam explained, trying not to laugh at the way Rosa had described them. "You walked in when I was making them."

"Oh, when you were rolling in flour," Mike recalled, nodding.

"What?" Alma asked, leaning forward a little to look at her face.

Alma was sitting on Sam's other side. The baby she was carrying was so large it didn't allow her to sit as close to the table as she would have wanted.

"Long story. You had to be there," Mike told her, and he was not about to elaborate at this time.

"Obviously," Cash, Alma's husband, laughed, adding his two cents in.

"It's a dessert," Sam explained to anyone who might have been curious. She looked at Alma. "It's really very light." She didn't add that she had made them one year for Christmas as a Christmas present for her mother, since there was very little money to be had for things like presents.

"Very light," Ray repeated. "To balance out Rosa's very heavy apple pie." When the housekeeper began to say something, Ray laughed, then jumped to his feet to hug the woman who had partially raised him, pressing a kiss to her cheek. It was how he always disarmed her. "You know I love you, Rosa."

"You sit down and behave yourself if you want to show me how much you love me," the woman ordered, pretending to scowl at him.

"Same old Rosa, all bark, no bite." Gabe laughed, shaking his head.

The look the older woman gave him had Gabe holding up his hands in complete surrender just as Mike had done earlier that day.

"If you are all finished, I would like to begin before all this is cold," Miguel said, calling for silence. The next moment, the din disappeared as if it had never been there.

Satisfied, the head of the Rodriguez family began. "Please, join hands and close your eyes," he instructed. When they did and he had taken Sam's hand in his right and Gabe's wife's hand in his left, in a clear, reverent voice, Miguel addressed his departed wife. "Another year has passed without you. I hope you are proud of these children you and I brought into the world. They miss you. But no one misses you as much as I do. Watch over them and me, so we can remain safe until such a time as the good Lord is ready to reunite us.

"God," he continued, "we thank you for all our good fortune. And thank you for watching over my children and blessing them with good people to love them," Miguel concluded.

As he did so, he glanced toward his oldest son before turning his attention to the turkey that was waiting in front of him.

"Let the slicing begin," Ray quipped as his father rose to his feet, picking up his carving knife and fork.

Sam could have sworn she felt her mouth watering as she watched the knife slide into turkey.

THE CELEBRATION FELT as if it went on forever—and yet it all but whirled by. Sam wouldn't have complained if it continued for a few hours more.

But everything, she knew, good or bad, had to eventually come to an end.

She shouldn't be greedy, she told herself. Instead, she should be grateful for this glimpse into what it was like to spend a holiday with a warm, loving family who might have been a tad too loud for some people, but every decibel of whose noisiness just throbbed of love as far as she was concerned.

The best thing about it was that for a little while, Sam knew she could actually say she was part of it. She'd been included in the conversations and in the preparation, and her efforts in decorating the dining room had been greatly appreciated and admired. Even a couple of Miguel's sons had commented on it.

Alma had expressed surprise that her father had done such festive decorations. When it was pointed out that the whole idea had been Sam's doing, Alma nodded and said, "I should have realized that it was her. The rest of you don't have a single artistic bone in your bodies," she said to her father and brothers.

As for Sam, after the meal, since she was forbidden even to rinse out so much as one glass, she found herself getting to know some of Mike's sisters-in-law and his nieces and nephews, despite the fact that the latter group consisted of very young children.

Talking to the children only brought home how much she loved children and how much she had hoped, back when she had been married to Danny, that she would become a mother.

But, just like with married life, it just wasn't meant to be for her, she thought, trying very hard to be philosophical and accepting about it. There was no point in being angry or upset about the absence of motherhood. Anger never resolved any situation.

All she could do—all anyone could do—was savor all the contact that came her way and be grateful that she at least had that—for however long she did.

Chapter Fifteen

"So, how's the book coming?" Mike asked.

Sam slanted a glance at him. The question seemed to come out of nowhere as they stood in front of the ranch house, watching Alma struggle to seat herself comfortably—or as comfortably as she could—in the passenger side of Cash's gray sedan.

Cash, meanwhile, was hovering over her, ready to help in any way he could and appearing helplessly clueless as to what that could possibly be.

"It's going well," Sam replied evasively.

She didn't want to talk about the book she was putting together for Mike's father. Didn't want to talk about the fact that she had it almost all worked out because that meant that her days here were numbered.

She blocked it all from her mind. This was a day for enjoying families, even if they were borrowed, as it was in this case. Tomorrow would be time enough to focus on the solitary life that was waiting for her once she finally put this project to bed.

Even so, she felt a small, icy shiver shimmy down her back.

Wanting to change the subject, she commented on

Alma's expression. "Your poor sister looks so grossly uncomfortable."

Mike laughed shortly. "That's probably because she is," he guessed. "Alma's problem was always trying to keep the weight on, not off." He remembered being surprised as a kid at what a strong punch his sister had since she had the dimensions and body mass of a stick. "She's never been this heavy before and even though I know she already loves the baby, she really hates being pregnant. I think she's literally counting the minutes until this baby arrives," he told her.

Instead of getting into the car once he finally got his wife seated and buckled up, Cash crossed back to where they were standing.

"Forget something?" Mike asked his brother-in-law, although he couldn't think of anything they had left behind.

"Not me, but Alma wanted me to ask you to write down the recipe for those white cakey things you made," Cash told the woman standing beside Mike. "She really liked them."

Sam grinned. He couldn't have said anything better to her if he'd tried.

"Sure, no problem. I can drop the recipe off at the sheriff's office tomorrow," she told Alma's husband. If it wasn't so late, she would have gone in search of paper and pen and jotted the recipe down right now.

"You getting any rest?" Mike asked Cash. His brother-in-law appeared exceedingly frazzled and worn around the edges to him, like someone sitting on a bomb and waiting for it to detonate.

Cash shrugged, apparently not bothering to deny the obvious. "Yeah, some," he mumbled.

"Get more," Mike told him firmly. "Because once that baby gets here, you can forget about resting for the next nine months to a year. Maybe longer."

Sam looked at him in surprise. Mike spoke with such authority, as if he knew exactly what to expect. A question suddenly materialized.

"You have kids?" she asked.

It never occurred to her that he might have been married at one point and that he was a father. No one had ever mentioned that, but then, it was his business and although this was a very loving family, she noticed they made a point of not invading each other's spaces.

"No, I have siblings," Mike countered. "And I remember when each one of them was born. It was the same with all five of them. Lots of crying, lots of noise, lots of diapers. *Especially* with the twins, Gabe and Rafe. And as I remember, there was no sleep to speak of. I think my parents ran on batteries for *months*. So rest up now, Cash. Memories of sleep are about all you're going to have soon."

"Cash?" Alma called, rolling down the window on the passenger side. "Is my brother trying to scare you?" she asked suspiciously.

"Just trying to get him prepared, Alma," Mike called back.

Cash squared his shoulders as he began to head back to his vehicle. "Guess it's too late to change our minds," he assumed.

"Not that you want to," Alma told him. "Right?" she added uncertainly.

"Nope," Cash told her as he got in behind the steering wheel.

"Well, pregnancy hasn't changed Alma any," Mike observed, watching his brother-in-law's car as it pulled away from the house and slowly disappeared down the road back to town. "She's still telling everyone what to think."

"Something you'd never do," Sam said, doing her best to keep a straight face.

That was the last of them. His brothers and their wives were all on their way home, each couple bundled off with enough leftovers to recreate another Thanksgiving dinner. Ray had already left for what he termed "a late date" and Miguel had excused himself just a little while ago and gone to bed.

Even Rosa, tired out by her long day, had retreated to her living quarters.

That had left the two of them to bid everyone else goodbye.

It was the perfect end to a perfect day, Sam couldn't help thinking as they turned around to go back into the house.

"By 'well,'" Mike said, picking up the thread of the conversation he'd begun earlier, "do you mean that you're able to read all the entries in the journals, or that you're almost finished putting it all in chronological order, or...?"

"Why? Are you that anxious to see me go?"

Under normal circumstances, he would have given Sam a flippant answer, one that by no means allowed her to suspect what he was thinking or how he felt about the situation.

But it was the tail end of a very long day that had turned out rather special when he reexamined it. Watching his siblings—Ray notwithstanding—Mike came to the very obvious conclusion that he was missing something. Something that in years past he would have just dismissed—or accepted.

But today, he found himself envying his siblings. Found himself wanting what they all had: someone to love who loved them in return. Although he'd gone out on occasion, he'd never met that "someone," that special person who made everything else so worthwhile.

And somewhere during the course of the day and evening that followed, amid the eating, the talking and the laughter, it suddenly occurred to Mike that he was blindly overlooking what was right in front of him.

That "someone" who completed him.

It was that feeling, that realization, that had him saying what he did in response to Sam's question. "No, I'm not. I'm not anxious at all to see you leave," he told her, his voice low and quietly sweeping along her upturned face.

His eyes holding hers, he lightly buried his fingers in her hair, cupped the back of her head and ever so gently tilted it up.

Bringing her face closer to his.

Sam could almost hear her heart pounding as everything around her seemed to stand still and hold its breath.

She waited.

Waited for that magical moment of contact.

And *prayed* that she wasn't waiting in vain.

She wasn't.

The next moment, his lips touched hers and all the emotions that she had kept bundled up inside of her, ready to bury, suddenly erupted inside of her. The next thing she knew, she wasn't just savoring Mike's kiss, she was kissing him back.

Hard.

With feeling.

Without realizing just how it happened, she found that her arms wove themselves around the back of his neck and her body leaned into his as one kiss fed into another. And then another after that, each one even more impassioned than the one that had come before.

Mike slipped his hand from the back of her head, dropped it down to her back as he pulled her into him, never breaking contact. Increasing the intensity of that contact until it would have taken an act of God to pull them apart.

She felt his body harden against hers. Felt her passion galvanizing within her.

Her head was spinning wildly as Sam fought the very strong desire to pull Mike's clothes away from his body, to shed her own so that there were no artificial barriers between them.

She knew that she should have been horrified that she was having these feelings, knew that she was acting completely out of character. Never in a hundred years would she have thought that she could be possessed by feelings this strong, by *needs* this overwhelming. Until this moment, she had always prided herself on her strength, on her control, born of her will to survive, never to be a victim of circumstances.

But right at this moment, she was weaker than she'd ever been, a leaf to be tossed about in the wind. Going somewhere she'd never been and no clue as to where that was.

Only that she desperately wanted to go there.

No one was more surprised than Mike when he felt himself reacting this way to this woman he hadn't even known existed a few short weeks ago. But from the first moment he had seen her, he'd felt something, known that she was different.

He had never encountered these feelings before.

He had already admitted to himself in the privacy of his own mind that he was attracted to her, that there was something about this puzzle of a woman that called to him, but he hadn't expected to react this strongly to her. After all, he had already kissed her before and while it had stirred him up, what he was feeling now was entirely unprecedented.

It felt, stripped down of all the bells and whistles, as if he was not able to breathe if he couldn't have her. If he couldn't be with her and possess her right now, body and soul.

Because she already possessed him that way.

The stillness in the house only amplified his need for this woman.

Before he knew what he was doing, Mike picked her up in his arms and carried her up the stairs.

If somewhere in his semi-consciousness, some small fragment of his mind expected her to pull away, to ask what he thought he was doing and call a halt to it all before it went any further, he was relieved that it didn't happen.

Instead her arms tightened around the back of his neck, as if she was fearful of breaking contact. And her mouth eagerly moved over his, drawing his very life out and feeding him an intoxicating stimulant that he had never tasted before.

His blood surged through his veins, his need for

her increasing just when he thought that wasn't humanly possible.

Mike found himself before her bedroom door.

This was where he set her down, gave her a chance to say no. Gave himself a chance to regroup, to think clearly.

It didn't happen.

Instead, still kissing her, he pushed the door open with his shoulder, crossed the threshold with her and then used his back to push the door back into place, closing them off from the rest of the house.

It was the "click" that did it. The lock moving into place. Almost silent, it still echoed through his head like the bells ringing in a church tower.

Mike pulled his lips away from hers.

He was breathless. They both were. He didn't know whether to apologize to her for the liberties he'd taken, the presumption he'd displayed.

Or just leave.

He did neither.

The look of raw desire and soul-twisting innocence he saw in her eyes wouldn't let him.

It reeled him back in.

The next moment, clothing began to fly as he pulled away her blouse, her simple skirt that had bedeviled him each time he watched her walk away, her hips moving in silent invitation.

Her bra was next to go, but not before Mike realized that she had stripped away his shirt and pulled off his jeans.

Sam tugged urgently at the latter because his muscular thighs impeded a quick removal.

As did his boots.

For a second time, his lips left hers as he pulled off first one boot, then the other, sitting on the floor as he did it so as not to lose his balance.

He lost his heart instead because from that vantage point, with Sam standing right before him, he drank in the arousing sight of her nude body and within less than a moment of his second boot hitting the floor, he'd pulled Sam back into his arms, his lips taking a second inventory of what his eyes had just seen.

Devouring her and at the same time, increasing his own hunger for her.

Mike was making her absolutely crazy. If she died right now, at this very moment, it would have been all right with her because, as near as she could calculate, she had already ascended into heaven.

She couldn't get enough of him. Mike had single-handedly caused every single inch of her to catch on fire. Everywhere he touched, everywhere his lips passed, became his and she eagerly returned the favor, familiarizing herself with his body the way she never had in the eighteen months that she had been married to her late husband.

That fact might have made her feel guilty if she hadn't been feeling so completely enthralled, so won-drously, utterly happy.

She had never been this happy, never felt this euphoric before.

Ever.

There'd been a section in the diaries she'd been reading where Marguerite, toward the end of her captivity, spoke of a strange longing that took hold of her, a longing she couldn't describe and swore she had never experienced before. It had to do with the warrior who was ultimately responsible for her escape.

When she had come across the passage and read it, Sam couldn't begin to understand the young woman's feelings or identify with her.

She could now.

Sparks all but flew as she felt Mike ever so lightly kissing the hollow of her throat, the side of her neck, trailing his lips along the swell of her breasts, possessing every tiny section of her even before he came to take her to that ultimate consummation.

And then it was happening.

Moving so that he was positioned over her on her bed, Mike laced his fingers through hers. His eyes held her a willing prisoner as his weight shifted and then she felt him joining her.

Becoming one with her.

The sensation was exquisite.

She drew in her breath as Mike began to move, at first slowly, then faster, increasing the tempo by degrees.

Sam was quick to match it, eagerly moving her hips in time with his, anticipating that last wonderful wave that promised to sweep them both to the edge of the universe.

She was desperate to have him feel what she was feeling.

The race increased, growing in speed, in magnitude, until that was all there was. It filled all the corners of her world.

She clutched his shoulders, thinking that it couldn't possibly be any better.

Until it was.

As a cry threatened to escape her lips, before she could press them together, Sam found Mike sealing her lips with his own.

The cry of exquisite fulfillment echoed from her mouth into his as she clung to Mike, digging her nails into his back, trying to hold on before she fell off the edge of the world, exhausted beyond words.

Chapter Sixteen

Gradually, as things like walls, the ceiling and basic surroundings began to return, defining the immediate world around them, Sam could almost feel herself falling back to earth.

When she was able to focus, she realized that she was lying beside Mike, cradled in the crook of his arm. A warm feeling continued to pervade through her.

The ordinarily solemn rancher had an unfathomable, somewhat bemused expression on his face. And he was looking directly at her.

Bracing herself for an answer she might not welcome, Sam still needed to ask what was behind his expression. "What?"

He laughed softly before answering, as if they were sharing a private joke. "I was just thinking that no one looking at you would ever guess that you could be such a tigress."

"A tigress," she echoed. She certainly had never been compared to *that* before, Sam thought. But then, she'd never felt like this before, either.

His eyes never left her face. "Uh-huh."

"Me?" she said, still not sure she'd actually heard him correctly.

The corners of his mouth curved and the smile entered his eyes. "Most definitely you."

"Well," she said, taking a deep breath, "I'm willing to bet that no one suspects how very gentle a lover you can be."

"Gentle." He'd been called a lot of things, some neutral, some not so neutral, but never gentle.

"That's the word," she replied, her own smile beginning to play on her lips.

"Don't know if I like that getting around," he told her. It wasn't exactly the kind of description a man strove to attain.

"Tell you what," she suggested, turning her body into his, "I won't tell if you don't."

"Deal." If she didn't know any better, she would have said that a devilish gleam had entered his eyes. "Besides, I'm more of a doer than a talker, anyway."

"Yes, I noticed," Sam agreed, her eyes never leaving his as she felt the excitement inside her building again, surprising her as much this time as it had the first time. "And just what is it you plan to do?" she asked innocently.

Mike shifted his weight and gathered her to him so that she was beneath him again. Every breath she took brought the contours of her body up against his, igniting a fresh flame.

"Guess," he challenged.

"Not good at guessing," she whispered, her heart hammering in her throat so hard she was having trouble swallowing.

"Then I guess I'll just have to show you," he concluded philosophically.

"Sounds good to me," she said just before her lips were suddenly covered, making her incapable of forming any more words.

Not that she wanted to.

AND SO IT BEGAN.

Rather than having the interlude mark the end to a perfect day, the threshold that was crossed in Sam's bedroom was the beginning of a new chapter of her life.

She knew that it would be a short one, but even so, she was going to savor every passage, every word.

To that end, during the day, fueled by a new energy, Sam worked diligently on the diaries she was transcribing and organizing into a coherent, entertaining whole. Moreover, the anticipation she experienced about the nights to come gave her a new, deeper insight into the mind and life of the woman whose words she was reading.

Sam could understand now what she'd puzzled over before. She could literally *feel* Marguerite's dilemma as the woman wrote about feeling disloyal to the dead youth who had previously owned her heart and had died on the day of her abduction. Disloyal because she began to have feelings, *intense* feelings, for the young Navajo brave who had become part of her life.

Her nights with Mike helped her see that Marguerite, almost against her will, had struck up more than just a friendship with the brave.

Reading between the lines, Sam realized that the young captive was in love with and had slowly formed a relationship with the warrior who ultimately helped her escape and get back to her own people.

I am caught between two worlds, part of both, part of none. I know I must choose between them and yet I desperately do not want to.

The passage almost seemed to stand out and glow before her when Sam came to it.

It could have been written by her.

Sam pressed her lips together as she sighed. "I know how you feel," she whispered to the page and to the spirit of the woman who had written it. "But at least you got to choose. I don't have that kind of a choice."

Everyone had been friendly and welcoming in Forever, as well as here on the ranch, but she had no illusions about her situation. No one was offering her a life here. They were just making the time that she spent here exceptionally pleasant.

But she was well aware that there was an end to her time here and it was drawing closer with each minute that passed by.

And she had somewhere else to be once she wrapped up her work here. She knew that for a fact.

Her publisher, Ethan Hawkins, had called yesterday to give her what he referred to as "the good news." Initially, she thought he was calling just to get an update on how she was coming along, but then she discovered there was another reason for the call, as well.

"Got another project lined up for you once you put this baby to bed," Hawkins told her. "Seems word is getting around about you, Sam." She could literally hear the smile in his voice. Hawkins had a wide, wide smile. "People other than me think you have a nice touch, professional but still down to earth. I took the liberty of talking to your agent before I called you. I think you'll be pleasantly surprised when he calls you. It's a really good offer."

She knew he was talking about the money, but her mind wasn't on that.

"How soon do I have to get started?" she asked. She was having trouble breathing. Her heart felt like lead in her chest.

"The sooner you finish up on what you're working on, the better," Hawkins told her. "They want you on the East Coast the minute you're done. Why?" he asked suspiciously. "You need some time off? Or is there a problem you didn't tell me about?"

All the other times, she'd been eager to take on the details of another project on the heels of the one she was completing. It kept her busy, kept her from thinking about anything other than her work. But this time was different. But she couldn't own up to it. Publishers didn't relish complications, only the end results.

She forced herself to sound upbeat, even as her heart was sinking. "No, no problem, just trying to work out a schedule in my head."

Still, Hawkins sounded unconvinced. "I thought you'd be more excited about this."

"I am," she was quick to assure the man. "I'm just a little tired, that's all." She grasped at the first excuse she could think of. "I haven't been getting much sleep lately."

And she hadn't, but it wasn't for the reason she was sure the publisher assumed. It was because the nights brought her more happiness than she thought was humanly possible and she didn't want to miss a moment of what was happening. Any time she spent sleeping was time she *wasn't* spending with Mike.

"You work too hard, Sam. Don't burn yourself out," Hawkins warned. "There are big things on your horizon," he promised mysteriously, then ended the conversation with, "Call me when you're ready to leave. I'll have Mavis make your travel arrangements," he said, referring to his secretary.

With that, Hawkins hung up.

Sam stared at her cell phone for a long time after she'd hit End. The word, she couldn't help thinking, was lamentably appropriate.

"WHERE ARE YOU tonight?" Mike asked her that night as they lay in her bed. As usual, the rest of the house was asleep, the way it always was before they quietly claimed their time together.

"Right here," Sam answered, doing her best to force a lightness into her voice that she didn't feel.

Mike propped himself up on his elbow to look down into her face. "No, you're not. What's wrong?"

"Well, for one thing," she said in a deliberately flippant tone, "the guy I'm trying to make love with is too talk-y."

He stopped her before she could get too carried away with the charade she was putting together. "Sam, one of the things I really like about you is that you don't lie. I realize now it's because you're so lousy at it, but the bottom line is that you don't lie. Or didn't." Mike looked very serious as he said, "Don't start now."

Sam blew out a breath. "Okay, I won't." She wasn't going to say anything until tomorrow morning, thinking they could have one more night together pretending that this could go on indefinitely. But obviously she hadn't counted on the fact that she was incredibly transparent. "My publisher called today."

"And?"

Mike's voice dropped down an octave, along with his heart, as he sensed that things were about to change from this moment on. He tried to tell himself that it was okay, that he'd known that what they had was just temporary and because of that, he'd been able to throw caution to the wind. He'd been able to be unrestricted in his reaction to her because the threat of commitment wasn't part of the equation.

The fact that he felt as if he'd just been punched in the gut was something he wasn't able to factor in.

Sam paused for a minute, trying to pull herself together before she continued. "And he has a new assignment for me."

"That's good, right?" he managed to say.

Is it? she silently demanded. *Are you happy to know that I won't be here soon? Why aren't you upset? Didn't any of this mean anything to you?*

"Right," she answered, her voice hollow, her mouth so dry she thought the word was going to get stuck before she could get it out.

"But we still have tonight, don't we?" Mike asked her softly.

She should be angry, hurt. She should walk away from him *now,* but all she could think of was that she wanted to make love with him one more time. One *last* time.

"We still have tonight," she agreed.

He took her back into his arms. "Then let's make the most of it."

She made love with abandon that last night, fully aware that there would be no more tomorrows, no more nights to look forward to.

Aware, too, that it didn't seem to make a difference to Mike because he hadn't even offered a single word in protest, hadn't said so much as, "Can't you stay a little longer?"

Nothing.

Was all she was to him was a warm, willing body? And who would occupy that space after she was gone? Would he even think of her once in a while after she'd left?

"Sam?" he said uncertainly, drawing back just as their lovemaking was reaching a fever pitch. He thought he'd felt something damp against his cheek. He looked at her closely. "Are you crying?"

"No," she protested with conviction. "I've got allergies," she lied. "They're acting up."

A hint of suspicion entered his voice. *Was* she crying? Was she upset because she was leaving? Had all this meant something to her, too? "I didn't know you had allergies."

"A lot of things about me you don't know," she replied, even as she felt herself closing off from him. From the world in general. It was safer that way. "I don't feel like talking tonight," she told him.

Then, before he could ask anything else, she began making love to him not just as if this was the last time, but as if all of life was over after this one final time—

because to her, it was—and it killed her to know that it probably didn't mean the same to him.

MIKE MADE HIMSELF scarce the next day, deliberately keeping away from Sam because he knew she was packing up and preparing to leave the ranch. She'd made it clear to him last night that today was her last day.

He wanted no part of it.

He'd walked out of the house before she had a chance to tell anyone else that she was leaving.

MIGUEL RECEIVED THE news of her pending departure with sorrow and made no effort to hide it from her.

"You have become part of our family in a very short time, Samantha," he told her when she broke the news. "I want you to remember that there will always be a place for you here at my table and in my house." Ordinarily, he tried not to interfere in other people's lives. But there was a great deal at stake here. "Are you sure that you must go?"

Sam nodded, willing her voice not to crack. Forbidding herself to cry. "My publisher said they wanted me working on this project as soon as possible."

"And you have to *go* where this project is?" Miguel questioned. "You cannot work on it from, say, right here?" he asked hopefully.

"It's better if I'm right there with the person whose autobiography I'm doing," she told him with a half-hearted smile.

"Better," he repeated, "but not all that necessary, yes? You could, perhaps, take many notes, then go somewhere else to write them, like perhaps, here again?" he asked.

The look in the older man's eyes slashed at her heart. Why couldn't Mike look at her that way? Why couldn't he protest a little? She didn't want him to lie down in front of her like a roadblock, but he could have at least said something about not being happy about her leaving.

"You're not making this easy for me, Miguel." She laughed.

"Good, because seeing you leave will not be easy for me," he told her. "I have come to think of you as a daughter," he continued seriously, "and, if I am not mistaken, you have come to think of all of us as a family perhaps?"

The way he said it, it sounded like half a question, half an assertion.

There were tears in Sam's eyes as she separated herself from the man. She still had to pack. "Please, Miguel, I have to go."

Miguel nodded. "I understand," he said sadly. "I will leave you to your packing." With that, he turned from her in the dining room and walked away, moving as if the weight of the world was on his shoulders, threatening to bend him in two.

MIGUEL WAS QUICK to inform the others what was going on. And to mention the fact that Mike seemed to have pulled a vanishing act.

The others fanned out to find him.

Eli turned out to be the lucky one. Or not so lucky as the case might be.

"What did that wood ever do to you?" Eli asked,

coming up behind his older brother on the other side of the barn.

In an effort to work out the frustration he was feeling over what was happening, Mike had decided to take out his aggression on the firewood.

"Nothing. I decided we needed to stock up on firewood," he said in between swings that seemed to vibrate all through him.

"It looks like you've got enough there to last through the blizzard of 2020, provided it actually decides to snow here," Eli commented, looking at the piles of firewood Mike had already chopped.

"Is there a point to this nonconversation?" Mike asked, annoyed that he couldn't be left alone. "Because if there isn't, I'd like to get back to what I'm doing."

Eli eyed him knowingly. "You mean wallowing in denial?"

Mike swung the ax again, making contact with a new cord of wood.

"Go away, Eli," he growled.

Rather than leave, Eli leaned against the side of the barn, crossing his arms before him and looking for all the world as if he intended to remain where he was.

"Not until you talk to me and tell me what's really wrong."

Mike slanted an exasperated look in his direction. "You mean other than having a nosy brother who won't back off?"

"Yeah, other than that."

Swallowing a curse, Mike set the ax to the side for a moment and glared at Eli. He might as well tell him. Of all his siblings, Eli was the one who could be trusted to keep things to himself.

"Okay, you asked for it." The words came tumbling out, confused and out of order, but maybe it was enough to satisfy his brother.

This wasn't easy, but he forced himself to talk about it. "You know how sometimes you see someone and your gut gets all twisted up and you don't even know why?"

To his surprise, Eli was smiling. "So she's got your gut all twisted up, does she?"

He should have realized this was a mistake, Mike thought. "She?" he repeated, a defensive edge in his voice.

Eli shook his head. "Yeah, 'she.' Sam," he clarified—as if he had to. "I know that you sure as hell weren't just talking about the way you feel about your horse. You've known him for a long time and this is the first time we're having this conversation, so it's about a woman. *The* woman," he underscored.

"We're not having this conversation," Mike announced, picking up the ax again.

"Look, what you just described as a twisted gut only comes along once in a lifetime—if that," Eli emphasized. "And if it does and you don't do anything about it—"

"Yeah? What?" Mike demanded. "If I don't do anything about it, then what?"

"Then you're a damn jackass if you don't go tell her how you feel," Eli concluded heatedly. "Because you're never going to feel like this about another woman again."

Mike didn't exactly see it that way. "I'll feel like a

jackass if I tell her and she still leaves," he fired back at his younger brother.

"But at least you would have tried," Eli insisted. He put his hand on Mike's shoulder, trying to get through to him. "What's the worst thing that can happen if you go talk to her? She leaves? Well, she's leaving now, isn't she? The way I see it, the only thing you're risking by telling her how you feel is getting her to stay."

Angry, confused and utterly torn, Mike put the ax down again. "You're not going to shut up until I go talk to her, are you?"

Eli grinned. "You know, you're not as dumb as you look."

Disgusted, Mike muttered something under his breath as he began to stride toward the house.

"Oh, and Mike," he called out, raising his voice, "about that winning personality of yours—"

Mike turned and looked at his brother over his shoulder. "Yeah?"

"Leave it out here," Eli suggested. "You'll do a lot better without it."

Mike bit off a response that rose to his lips. He didn't have any more time to waste out here, talking to Eli. He had a woman he needed to convince to stay in a town that was no bigger than a tear.

Chapter Seventeen

Sam had always made it a point to travel light for a reason. That way, she could be packed and ready to go in no time at all.

It was taking longer this time. Longer because of all the memories that were going into the suitcase along with her clothes. Her suitcase didn't seem to be big enough to hold all of them.

As for packing up her actual clothing, that should have been a snap. It always had been before.

But this time, she was moving in slow motion. It was, she thought, remembering a description her mother had once used, as if she had glue in her veins. Glue that had already dried.

Consequently, she was less than half done when she heard the light knock on her door.

"Door's not locked."

Feeling her heart accelerating, Sam turned around in time to see Olivia and Angel peering into her room before entering. She wasn't sure who she was more surprised to see, the sheriff's wife, who was also one of the town's attorneys, or Gabe's new bride, the chef who Miss Joan swore by.

"May we come in?" Olivia asked. She and Angel were still on the other side of the bedroom's threshold.

"Sure. You don't need my permission," Sam told them. "This isn't even going to be my room in an hour."

That was how much longer she had here, Sam thought. An hour. Sixty short minutes and then this was all going to be behind her.

Just the very thought made her heart ache.

"That's kind of what we came to see you about," Angel told her in her quiet cadence. "Gabe's father called us. Miguel thought that maybe between the two of us, Olivia and I might be able to talk you into staying a little while longer."

Sam noticed that Olivia had moved her open suitcase from the bed onto the desk and then she and Angel sat down in the newly vacated space.

"Really, I'd love to," Sam began to explain.

Hearing what she wanted to hear, Olivia was quick to interrupt in hopes of cutting off anything that might come after that initial assertion. "Then there's no problem," she declared.

"But I can't," Sam said firmly, concluding her sentence. "I've finished what I was sent here to do."

She'd intentionally dragged her feet, but it was finally done. She'd even left a rough draft of her finished product for Miguel to read over once she left. She intended to drop him a note to let him know where to find the draft. It was easier that way. She couldn't bear having him go over the reworked diary, into which she had put more than a piece of herself, while she was anywhere near him.

"And I've got another book lined up to work on," she told the women.

"And you can't work on the book from here?" Olivia asked.

Sam shook her head, not allowing herself to even entertain that possibility. Her method was to always be hands-on. She'd never worked any other way and she couldn't think about switching now. What was the point? Mike didn't really seem to care if she stayed or went.

"No."

"Not even with Skype and all the advantages of modern conferencing?" Olivia pressed.

"No," Sam assured her firmly. "Look, I had a really wonderful time here and believe me, if I could stay, I would, but—"

"Would you?" Olivia interrupted, the lawyer in her coming to the foreground as she questioned Sam.

Sam said nothing. There was no point in arguing about this. She had to leave and it didn't matter if the whole town came to try to talk her into remaining. The one person who should be talking to her hadn't said a single meaningful word on the subject.

"Miguel felt we were the best equipped to talk to you about staying because we each had to make a choice to remain in Forever or go back to the world that we came from," Angel told her. "Olivia was a partner in a large criminal law firm and well on her way to the top while I had a pretty good career going myself," she added modestly without elaborating. "We chose happiness over material things and neither one of us have ever regretted it," she concluded with feeling.

It was a lovely story, Sam thought, but it had nothing to do with her. Both women remained because the men they loved had come forward to ask them to stay.

That wasn't the case with her.

She was about to beg off, saying she was running behind when the women tag-teamed her again and Olivia started talking once more.

"Think about what your leaving is going to do to Mike," she warned.

Sam didn't bother trying to stifle her laugh. Her leaving would do less than nothing to Mike if the past twelve hours was anything to go on.

"I'm sure he'll be fine. When I told him I was leaving last night, he just took it in stride," she told them in a lofty tone that was meant to hide the hurt beneath. "It's obviously no big deal for him."

Olivia fixed her with a disappointed look. "Really? I thought you were more observant than that."

"There's nothing to observe," Sam told her crisply. "Mike wasn't even around this morning."

She'd woken up to an empty bed and an emptiness inside of her that felt like an insurmountable chasm. Only when she came down to breakfast did she find out that he was already out, doing "chores." As far as she was concerned, Mike's main "chore" was avoiding her.

She didn't want a man who would rather disappear than try to fight for her, at least verbally.

"A man like Mike has trouble showing his emotions," Angel tried to tell her. "That doesn't mean he doesn't have them."

"That doesn't mean that he does, either," Sam countered.

"That's where you're wrong," Angel insisted softly. "Everyone in the family's noticed that he's gotten friendlier, happier and less serious, especially since Thanksgiving."

Was it her imagination, or was Angel looking at her pointedly?

"You leave," Olivia warned, "and he's going to come apart at the seams."

Sam sincerely doubted that. "Oh, he's a lot more resilient than you're giving him credit for," she assured the sheriff's wife.

"Ordinarily, I'd say yes, but in this case, I've got some very real doubts. People like Mike and me don't give our hearts easily, but when we do, it's forever. Haven't you noticed that he's different now than he'd been when you first got here?"

Sam shrugged, feeling helpless. There was probably a logical explanation for that.

"Maybe," she allowed

"No 'maybe' about it," Olivia told her with conviction. "Think about it," she urged Sam, giving her arm a squeeze. "You really don't want to do something you're going to live to regret."

Turning, she nodded at Angel and then she and Angel withdrew, leaving Sam to contemplate the inside of her half-filled suitcase, feeling as if she was damned if she left and damned if she stayed. But sticking to a schedule had seen her through the worst of times and she deliberately had a schedule to stick to now.

So hop to it, Sam. Stop being so mopey. You had a good time, you wrote a good book, now go before you ruin everything by being clingy.

With a sigh, Sam began packing again only to once more be interrupted by yet another knock on her door.

Humor curved her lips ever so slightly. They just didn't give up, did they?

"What did you forget to say?" she asked before turning toward the doorway to see, she assumed, Olivia and Angel returning.

Except that wasn't what she saw at all.

"I forgot to say 'Don't go.'"

Sam's eyes widened as she stared at him. "Mike?"

"Don't tell me you've forgotten what I look like already," Mike said flippantly, walking in. "You haven't even left yet."

The words weren't coming, as if stuck on flypaper in her head. When she finally spoke, it was almost haltingly.

"I didn't forget. I'm just—stunned, I guess, for lack of a better word. Who put you up to this?" she asked.

He looked at her, confused. "What?"

Okay, maybe she was talking too fast. She had a tendency to do that when she became agitated. Sam tried again.

"Angel and Olivia were just here. They said that I shouldn't go because, well, just because," she said, thinking it best not to embarrass him with details that probably weren't true anyway. "Your father asked them to talk to me. Did he talk to you about this, about my leaving?" she asked.

Mike shook his head. "No."

She thought of the other possibility. "Then did they talk to you? Olivia and Angel," she said to refresh his memory.

"Not since Thanksgiving," he told her. He knew what she was thinking. That he wouldn't have come here on his own. Apparently he had some surprises left up his sleeve. "Why?" he asked her. "Don't you think I can think for myself?"

"Sure, just not about—" Oh, hell, her tongue was getting tied up in a knot. "Damn it, this is really awkward."

"Then let me make it less awkward," Mike volunteered. When she started to say something, he laid his finger against her lips to silence her. "I know you have to work, I know that this is what you like to do. I've walked in on you while you were working often enough to see that you look as if you're practically glowing. I'm not going to ask you to give that up."

So much for that, she thought, dejected. She did her best to mask her feelings. "Okay then, I'd better finish packing."

As she turned toward the suitcase, he caught her arms and turned her back around to face him. "But I am going to ask you to come back."

She stared at him as if he'd suddenly started to talk in a strange language. "What?"

"I'm going to ask you to come back," he repeated. "And to keep coming back." His eyes held hers as he added, "To me."

Her breath backed up in her throat. But she was afraid to believe what she thought he was saying. There had to be another explanation.

"And why should I do that?" she asked, her voice sounding deceptively quiet.

Okay, here it was, all or nothing, Mike thought. But if he didn't risk it, there was no chance of winning all the marbles.

So he risked it.

"Because I'm asking you to. Because I love you and because if I had to deal with a world without you in it for the rest of my life, that life wouldn't go on for very long."

She wasn't sure what to say, other than his name. So she started there. "Mike—"

He didn't want her to turn him down, didn't want to hear her say "no" to him. Taking her hands in his, he held on to them and pleaded his case as best he could, fervently wishing he had his brother-in-law's gift of stating things. Like Olivia, Cash was an attorney.

"Rafe's wife, Val, works part-time as a location scout for the movies, the rest of the time she's a professional photographer. She travels around, but her home base is here. No matter where she goes, Rafe knows it's just temporary and she'll come back here. To Forever. And to him. It's not the ideal situation, but it's better than doing without her completely. I think that maybe having to live without her for stretches of time makes him appreciate her even more."

They were circling the subject and she wanted a direct hit. "And you're suggesting what?"

He summarized it for her. And crossed his fingers.

"That you do what you have to do to be happy, just promise you'll come back to me every time a job is finished."

Her expression remained the same as she studied him, gauging the sincerity of his sentiment. "And you'd be satisfied with that?"

"I'd have to be," he said philosophically. "The bottom line is that I want you to do whatever it takes to make you happy. Because if you're happy, then I'm happy." He couldn't believe he was actually saying that. But it was true. And he meant every word of it. "As long as I can see you and be with you once in a while, it'll be okay."

"But maybe living like that won't make me happy," she told him.

"Oh." She was saying she didn't want to come back here, he thought, his heart sinking.

"Maybe living here full-time is what'll make me happy," she went on. It was obvious that her answer confused Mike, she could see it in his face and she surrendered the serious expression she was trying to maintain. Instead, she laughed. "Let me try to explain this better. When Danny died, I came apart and desperately searched for something to keep me busy, to keep me from thinking how alone I was. I lucked into ghostwriting. I love to write, but a career as a ghostwriter was never my main goal. Keeping sane was.

"It recently struck me that maybe your weekly paper could use a little punching up, maybe an online blog to keep people up-to-date with things that are going on. Sort of like an online version of Miss Joan," she added with a grin.

"That means you'd be staying here." He said the words slowly, as if he was tasting each one, all the while watching her face to see if he had made a completely baseless assumption.

But he hadn't, he realized, because Sam asked, "You have a problem with that?"

"Me?" He stared at her, almost not comprehending the words coming out of her mouth. "God, no. I can't think of anything better, except for maybe one thing."

She braced herself for anything. "And that is?"

"If you agreed to marry me."

For a second, she couldn't say a word because in addition to not being able to breathe, she thought that she was dreaming.

When she could finally speak, Sam uttered only one word. "When?"

This was real, Mike thought. She was going to stay. She was actually going to stay. The relief he felt was unbelievable—and overwhelming.

"Whenever you're ready," he replied.

"I've always thought that Christmas was a nice time for a wedding. Too soon?" she asked.

He grinned, taking her into his arms. "Not soon enough." This meant, he thought, that he was going to have to make Eli his best man. Because if it hadn't been for Eli, he would have still been behind the barn, chopping cords of wood and turning them into twigs at this point. "But I guess I can wait," he said philosophically. "And, I guess this way, it'll give us time to rehearse."

"The wedding?" she asked.

His eyes glinted as he corrected her. "The hon-eymoon."

Every inch of Sam was smiling as she said, "I think I can live with that."

"Yeah, me, too," Mike said just before he kissed her and sealed both their fates.

Happily.

* * * * *

Don't miss Marie's next
Harlequin American Romance,
THE COWBOY'S CHRISTMAS SURPRISE,
available in December 2013!

REQUEST YOUR FREE BOOKS!
2 FREE NOVELS PLUS 2 FREE GIFTS!

⊕ HARLEQUIN®

American ★ Romance®

LOVE, HOME & HAPPINESS

YES! Please send me 2 FREE Harlequin® American Romance® novels and my 2 FREE gifts (gifts are worth about $10). After receiving them, if I don't wish to receive any more books, I can return the shipping statement marked "cancel." If I don't cancel, I will receive 4 brand-new novels every month and be billed just $4.74 per book in the U.S. or $5.24 per book in Canada. That's a savings of at least 14% off the cover price! It's quite a bargain! Shipping and handling is just 50¢ per book in the U.S. and 75¢ per book in Canada.* I understand that accepting the 2 free books and gifts places me under no obligation to buy anything. I can always return a shipment and cancel at any time. Even if I never buy another book, the two free books and gifts are mine to keep forever.

154/354 HDN F4YN

Name	(PLEASE PRINT)

Address	Apt. #

City	State/Prov.	Zip/Postal Code

Signature (if under 18, a parent or guardian must sign)

Mail to the Harlequin® Reader Service:
IN U.S.A.: P.O. Box 1867, Buffalo, NY 14240-1867
IN CANADA: P.O. Box 609, Fort Erie, Ontario L2A 5X3

Want to try two free books from another line?
Call 1-800-873-8635 or visit www.ReaderService.com.

* Terms and prices subject to change without notice. Prices do not include applicable taxes. Sales tax applicable in N.Y. Canadian residents will be charged applicable taxes. Offer not valid in Quebec. This offer is limited to one order per household. Not valid for current subscribers to Harlequin American Romance books. All orders subject to credit approval. Credit or debit balances in a customer's account(s) may be offset by any other outstanding balance owed by or to the customer. Please allow 4 to 6 weeks for delivery. Offer available while quantities last.

Your Privacy—The Harlequin® Reader Service is committed to protecting your privacy. Our Privacy Policy is available online at www.ReaderService.com or upon request from the Harlequin Reader Service.

We make a portion of our mailing list available to reputable third parties that offer products we believe may interest you. If you prefer that we not exchange your name with third parties, or if you wish to clarify or modify your communication preferences, please visit us at www.ReaderService.com/consumerchoice or write to us at Harlequin Reader Service Preference Service, P.O. Box 9062, Buffalo, NY 14269. Include your complete name and address.

HAR13R

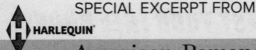
This was what Eve wanted, too. Even if she would have preferred not to admit it. Before she could stop herself, before she could think of all the reasons why not, she let Derek pull her closer still. His head dipped. Her breath caught, and her eyes closed. And then all was lost in the first luscious feeling of his lips lightly pressed against hers.

It was a cautious kiss. A gentle kiss that didn't stay gallant for long. At her first quiver of sensation, he flattened his hands over her spine and deepened the kiss, seducing her with the heat of his mouth and the sheer masculinity of his tall, strong body. Yearning swept through her in great enervating waves. Unable to help herself, Eve went up on tiptoe, leaning into his embrace. Throwing caution to the wind, she wreathed her arms about his neck and kissed him back. Not tentatively, not sweetly, but with all the hunger and need she felt. And to her wonder and delight, he kissed her back in kind, again and again and again.

Derek had only meant to show Eve they had chemistry. Amazing chemistry that would convince her to go out with him, at least once. He hadn't expected to feel tenderness well inside him, even as his body went hard with desire. He hadn't expected to want to make love to her here and now, in this empty house. But sensing that total surrender would be a mistake, he tamped down his own desire and let the kiss come to a slow, gradual end.

Eve stepped backward, too, a mixture of surprise and pleasure on her face. Her breasts were rising and falling quickly, and her lips were moist. Amazement at the potency of their attraction, and something else a lot more cautious, appeared in her eyes. Eve drew a breath, and then anger flashed. "That was a mistake."

Derek understood her need to play down what had just happened, even as he saw no reason to pretend they hadn't enjoyed themselves immensely. "Not in my book," he murmured, still feeling a little off balance himself. In fact, he was ready for a whole lot more.

Can Derek convince Eve to take a chance
on him this Christmas?

Find out in
THE TEXAS CHRISTMAS GIFT
by Cathy Gillen Thacker
Available December 3, only from
Harlequin® American Romance®.

Since the first grade, Holly Johnson has known that Ramon Rodriguez is the only man for her. But the carefree, determinedly single Texas cowboy with the killer smile doesn't have a clue. Until they share a dance and a kiss... and Ray finally sees his best friend for the woman in love she is. Now that he realizes what he's been missing, Ray plans to make up for lost time...starting with the three little words Holly's waited thirteen years to hear.

The Cowboy's Christmas Surprise
by *USA TODAY* bestselling author
MARIE FERRARELLA

Available November 5,
from Harlequin® American Romance®.